This book b

Children's
POOLBEG

Spike,
the Professor
and Doreen
in London

First published 1991 by
Poolbeg Press Ltd
Knocksedan House,
Swords, Co Dublin, Ireland

ISBN 1 85371 130 6

Cover design by Steven Hope
Set by The Set-Up, Sundrive Road, Dublin.
Printed by The Guernsey Press Ltd,
Vale, Guernsey, Channel Islands

Spike, the Professor and Doreen

in London

Tony Hickey

Children's
POOLBEG

*To Rita with admiration and
gratitude for all her help*

Contents

1	At the Tower	1
2	A Welcome Interruption	17
3	Talking with the Grown-Ups	29
4	At the Hotel	38
5	Taking Off	56
6	Regent's Park	64
7	London Town	74
8	What's Going On?	84
9	Alice Arrives	91
10	Brunhilde Runs Off	108
11	Trouble in Traffic	118
12	Brunhilde's Plan	129
13	At the Restaurant	137
14	Happy Endings	149

1
At the Tower

our young people sat on a seat in the shadow of the Martello Tower on Strand Road, Sandymount, Dublin. It was quite a crush but none of them seemed aware of this, any more than they were aware of the beauty of the morning or of the flocks of seabirds, feeding off the debris left by the departing tide. Not even the sun affected their gloomy silence as it sparkled off the sails of the racing yachts stretched in a long line on the horizon.

Brandy, the great shaggy dog, who lay at their feet, looked dolefully out across the sands. Ordinarily, on such a lovely day as this, he would be trying to catch gulls or looking for some driftwood to chew or, best of all, finding an old tyre that could become part of a great

game of push-and-roll with the help of his two
favourite boys.

But these two boys, jammed on one half of
the seat, continued to stare unseeingly into
the distance. The taller of the two, Spike (real
name Stephen Arthur Patrick O'Halligan),
had until this moment shown almost no wish
to sit still for any length of time, much less to
be so deeply lost in thought. But on this particular morning even the piece of hair from
which he got his nickname seemed to be affected by the general mood of gloom and just
drooped limply at the back of his head.

Next to Spike was the Professor (real name
Damien Hayden O'Neill), who owed his nickname, not just to his horn-rimmed glasses, but
also to the fact that his father really was a
professor. It was less unusual for him to sit
and think but Brandy had never known him to
do it so long or so deeply as this.

Doreen, Spike's sister, was next on the
bench. She was, perhaps, the most level-headed
of the group, seldom panicking, inclined to be
practical. Or, at least, she had been until the
arrival in Dublin of Brunhilde Brisk, who was
the fourth occupant of the bench.

Brunhilde had been born and raised in
Santa Fe, New Mexico, in the United States of

America, where not only her father but also her mother were professors at one of the universities.

The effect of Brunhilde on those who had got to know her since her plane touched down at Dublin Airport, could be compared to that of a hurricane on a peaceful landscape. Like a tall fair-haired Viking warrior, she had invaded the lives of the O'Halligans and the O'Neills, in whose house she was staying.

It must also be said that her parents, Ramon and Sandra, were not exactly quiet, faint-hearted people. On their very first morning, they had roused the whole neighbourhood at dawn by performing a dance of welcome to the sun with the help of a cassette of very loud drum music.

Mr Gilchrist, who lived four doors away from the O'Neills, had actually come around in his dressing gown, claiming that his family was frightened out of its wits, expecting at any moment to be attacked by a raiding party of Apaches.

The O'Neills all decided that this was just Mr Gilchrist's way of being sarcastic. As head of a large business, he would surely know that there were no Apaches in Dublin 4. Even if there were, they would be unlikely to try and take over the area in a dawn raid.

Anyway, the drum beat that the Brisks danced to didn't come from the Apache tribe. It had come from a wise old Indian in Santa Fe.

But, from that moment, things had got more and more out of hand with Brunhilde the driving force behind almost everything that happened.

Now, for the first time, she was as silent as her three Irish companions.

Brandy didn't mind her silence too much. In fact he rather welcomed it for he knew that she didn't like him. The very first time he had tried to welcome her to Ireland, she had screamed and screamed in a very alarming way.

The only other human that he knew for sure didn't like him was Mrs O'Halligan, mother of Spike and Doreen, but she at least disliked him in a nice, quiet way.

Whenever she saw him anywhere near her house in Irishtown, a short distance down the road from the Tower, she would look firmly at him and say, "That dog is not coming in here."

Brandy, in a way, understood this. It would be a very foolish dog indeed who would expect to be liked by every human being or even by every other dog. He had his own likes and dislikes just as he knew that Spike and the

Professor had theirs.

Spike's main dislike at the moment was Brunhilde, which was why he sat as far away from her as possible and kept Brandy as close to him as possible. That way he could be fairly certain of Brunhilde not wanting to hold his hand or tell him that he was "real cute," although, since their day at the races, Spike hoped that Brunhilde had turned her attention to none other than Scarce, lead singer with The Tree-Tops, currently at number one with their single "Down a Well."

Meeting Scarce had been like a dream come true for Brunhilde. She saw it as her big chance to become one of the world's great composers of pop-tunes. Her boast was that she could compose a tune to suit any occasion. This was, in a way, true, although Spike and the Professor both agreed that, while the words changed, the tune always seemed to be the same.

Not that this seemed to bother Brunhilde. In fact, nothing seemed to bother Brunhilde when it came to getting her own way. She was so full of confidence that it was positively disgusting. She claimed that she had inherited her musical talent from her mother, who lectured on music in Santa Fe, and her sense of history from her father, who taught history.

Her sense of her own talent she had acquired all by herself, with the full approval of her parents, who seemed to think that the sun rose and set in their daughter. Everything that Brunhilde said or did was all right with them or, at least, that was how it seemed until Mrs O'Brien, Spike's and Doreen's granny, had taken the young people to the race-meeting at the Curragh.

What had happened at that meeting now seemed to Spike like a strange, mixed-up dream where laughter and disaster played an equal part.

Fortunately everything had ended brilliantly with two of the world's most famous TV stars, Jenny South and Daly Carson, inviting them all to spend a weekend with them in London. Brunhilde had been particularly excited by the idea because Scarce had promised to listen to her songs the very first chance that he got. London would give him that chance.

Spike realised that Scarce had probably been counting on never seeing Brunhilde again and had made the promise just to get away from her. But the invitation from the TV stars to stay at their houses had given Brunhilde visions of herself seated at a piano, while

Scarce and The Tree-Tops gathered around and listened to her compositions. She was convinced that they would want to record all her songs immediately. They might even—and this was a possibility that she had talked about non-stop since Sunday morning—ask her to record some of the songs herself. She might—and here she had grinned generously—even include Spike and the Professor and Doreen as her backing group. "We could call ourselves Brunhilde and the Digitals," she declared.

Spike didn't want to be part of a pop-group if it meant being bossed around by Brunhilde, especially since she was bound to have some terrible idea of what they all ought to wear. She'd probably want them to dress up as watches, going "tick-tock" while she yelled into the microphone.

In spite of the heat of the day, Spike shivered at the idea of being completely under Brunhilde's thumb. Then he got a strange feeling of comfort at the thought that none of it might ever happen. But he thought sadly that he was not just thinking of Brunhilde and the Digitals when he thought of things not happening. He was also thinking of the entire trip to London not happening at all.

That was the reason that the four of them

were sitting there so silent and glum. Since
Daly and Jenny had issued their invitations,
nothing more had been heard from them.

At first, Brunhilde had refused to be worried
by this. As they drove back to Dublin on
Sunday, the day after the disco-party, she said,
"I think I'd better spend the rest of the afternoon sorting out my songs and also deciding
what clothes to take to London."

That had suited Spike and the Professor.
Even Doreen seemed to welcome some time
away from her new friend.

But the time away from Brunhilde had not
proved to be as carefree as Doreen and the two
boys imagined.

First of all, Doreen had to deal with Imelda
Flood, who used to regard herself as Doreen's
best friend. She had been on holiday in Greece
when the all-blonde American had arrived in
Dublin. She had been outraged to get back
home full of tales of life on the island of Kos
only to find that Doreen had had a much more
exciting time at the race meeting on the
Curragh, where she had met dozens of famous
people and as a result had been on television
and had her picture in all the newspapers.
Imelda had barely spoken to Doreen when
they met on Sunday afternoon. When

Brunhilde came out that evening, she had just stood listening to her.

The boys' problems arose with Winky Murphy and his gang. Winky was one of the toughest boys in their school, always in trouble, always pushing others around. In fact, if they ever got together, Brunhilde and Winky could have ruled the neighbourhood between them. But Winky was in no mood for power-sharing. Like Imelda Flood, he was jealous of the new-found fame of Spike and the Professor but didn't know what to do about it, apart from sneering when he met them.

When he read in the newspapers that Daly Carson and Jenny South had gone back to London, he had made a point of being outside the O'Halligan house in Irishtown when Spike left on the previous morning to meet the Professor.

"How are all your famous friends?" he'd asked while the members of his gang stood around and grinned.

"What's that to do with you?" demanded Spike, sensing that something worse than a scrap was about to happen.

"Oh we were just wondering if you'd heard from them or ever would again. My Mam says it was all just a publicity stunt and that you

have as much chance of getting to London as I
have of going to the moon."

"My mother says the same," said Imelda
Flood, who "just happened" to be passing.

"And what does your mother know about
it?" asked Doreen, who came out of the house
in time to hear her former best friend.

"She knows what she reads in the paper,"
Imelda replied, "which is very different from
what that nutter from Santa Fe has been going
around saying." Imelda threw her head and
her shoulders back and began to swing her
hips in what was quite a good imitation of
Brunhilde. When she spoke, she even had
Brunhilde's accent.

"Oh yes, when I and my friends go to dear
little old London to stay with our friends, Daly
and Jenny, we are going to become so well-
known and famous that you might never see
us in dear little old Dublin again."

The gang roared with laughter and hooted
and whistled to such an extent that Mrs
O'Halligan came to the front door to see what
was going on.

"Oh it's you," she said, when she saw Winky.

"Oh yes, Mrs O'Halligan, it is I and my
friends and dear little Imelda Flood come to
say farewell to dear little old Spike and

Doreen before they set out on their long
journey to the Martello Tower on Strand Road,
for that is as far as either of them will be
going." Winky's imitation of Brunhilde was
almost as good as Imelda's.

Before Mrs O'Halligan could think of a suitable reply, Winky and Imelda and the gang
rushed off, almost colliding with Mrs Moody,
arch-enemy of most young people in the district.

"Mind where you're going," Mrs Moody
snapped.

"There's a dead duck on your head," Winky
yelled back as he and the others turned the
corner.

Mrs Moody clapped her hands on top of her
head before she realised that it was to her new
hat that Winky was referring in that disres-
pectful way. "That's what comes from children
going to race-meetings." She glared at Mrs
O'Halligan and then went into the newspaper
shop, where she was very rude to the young
assistant.

"Don't mind her," Mrs O'Halligan said com-
fortingly to Spike and Doreen. "It'll be all
right."

But it wasn't all right. And looking back now
on the way their mother had spoken to them,

Spike could see that she had been trying to make them feel better but that, like Winky and his gang, she did not really believe that any of them would get to London.

When Mr O'Halligan got home from work that evening, his words had the same feeling to them. "You mustn't worry," he had said. "Jenny South and Daly Carson are very busy people. The invitation might have just slipped their minds."

But did that mean that the invitation had slipped their minds forever? Spike was suddenly prepared to dress up, not only as a watch, but as a grandfather clock and make any noise that Brunhilde wanted rather than have to put up with the mockery of Winky and his gang for the rest of the summer.

"It's not fair," Spike said out loud.

Brandy's ears pricked up. Could that break in the silence mean they were on the move at long last? Since the two boys had collected him from the yard at Miss Finucane's half-an-hour ago, they had only walked him as far as the Tower. He had been looking forward since first light to a wonderful gallop across the strand. But Spike's words, "It's not fair," just made the other three on the seat sigh and settle down even more firmly.

Brandy found that he had to sigh as well. He gave the Professor's hand a little lick to try and comfort him.

The Professor looked at him, managed a smile and stroked his ears.

At the same moment, there was the sound of the enemy approaching. Winky Murphy and his gang came yelling and shouting around the bend in Strand Road. Close behind them was Imelda Murphy, with several girls from Doreen's class. Imelda was carrying the small bouzouki she had bought in Greece.

It was perfectly obvious to the four on the seat that the sole purpose of the approaching group was to annoy them.

Brandy growled, by way of an offer to terrify Winky and his friends.

"No, Brandy, " the Professor said. "We're in enough trouble without you making it worse."

"Maybe we should move," said Spike.

"They'd only follow us," said the Professor.

"Why don't we just ignore them?" said Doreen. "Pretend that they don't exist."

That proved easier said than done as they were surrounded by grinning, smirking faces, who laughed even more when Imelda repeated her imitation of Brunhilde. "Oh yes, I and my parents are just the greatest people in the world. I and my parents are delighted to be able to number among our friends the O'Halligans and sweet little Professor O'Neill. Only, of course, my real boy-friend is pop-singer, Scarce, who has become so scarce that I may never never see him again."

A nerve began to twitch in Brunhilde's cheek.

Doreen thought, She's getting angry. Imelda is really upsetting her.

Winky joined in the mockery. "Oh but what about their great friends, Daly Carson and Jenny South, who are going to take them off to London, I don't think!"

Suddenly the twitching nerve stopped. Brunhilde stretched slightly and said to her three companions. "Did you ever hear the saying that in order to think you have to have a brain?"

Imelda Flood stretched as well and said, "Did you ever hear the saying that you have to have a brain to know what's true from what isn't true?"

"Jealousy can make the wisest person look foolish." Brunhilde smiled with terrible sweetness as she spoke.

Imelda's hand trembled slightly as she held on to her bouzouki. "Jealous? Who's jealous?

And of what?"

Brunhilde continued to stare calmly out to sea and still spoke as though quite unaware of the hostile crowd around her. "Do you smell fish? Stale fish?"

"We'll soon see who's smelly when you find out how the whole place is laughing at the lot of you," declared Winky. "Spike's mother will be ashamed to put her face out the door."

Spike's determination to remain calm vanished. So too did Doreen's.

"You leave my mother out of this," Spike said.

"And mine too," yelled Doreen as though they did not have the same mother. "Brunhilde is right. You are all jealous."

"Jealous of what?" demanded Imelda. "Jealous of the fact that this twerp from America has been going around telling stories about things that'll never happen? And don't think you can come back sucking up to me when she goes back to America!"

"And what makes you think I'll be leaving Doreen or Spike or the Professor behind me when I go back to America?" Brunhilde spoke directly to Imelda for the first time.

The two boys and Doreen exchanged alarmed glances. It was bad enough to be mocked over the London trip. What would it be like when Brunhilde actually did go back to Santa Fe and they were still in Dublin! They would never live that down!

Doreen tugged at Brunhilde's arm to warn her to say no more but Brunhilde pulled free and stood up, somehow managing to appear taller than usual. She was actually able to look down on Winky and Imelda and their companions. When she spoke, she spoke with the voice of a leader, facing a group of treacherous followers.

"I'm sorry if Imelda Flood thinks I am trying to make trouble between her and Doreen. This I have no wish to do. As for Winky here, I think perhaps he is a bully who has to be the leader, no matter what. Well, Winky, you may continue to be the leader of your gang as long as you stay well clear of me and my friends. We have greater and more important things to do than humour you."

The world seemed to hold its breath as Brunhilde finished speaking. Then the spell began to break as Winky realised that he had just been told to shove off. But before he could say anything, there was a screech of brakes on the road. A huge black car skidded to a stop, causing the cars and lorries behind to blow their horns.

2
A Welcome Interruption

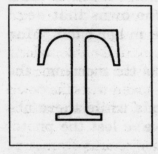 wo familiar figures got out of the car and waved at the young people. Spike was the first to recognise the man. "It's Martin Daly, all dressed up."

"Who's Martin Daly?" one of Imelda's group asked.

"Daly Carson's cousin. He's living near the Star of the Sea Church," Doreen said.

"And who's the woman with him?" another voice asked.

"That," said Brunhilde with a great note of triumph in her voice, "is Alice Hopper who looks after the publicity for The Tree-Tops." She and Doreen hugged each other. This unexpected interruption could be just what was needed. It could also mean positive news about going to London!

Alice Hopper began talking as soon as she was within earshot of the group. "So there you are! Mr. Daly and I have been looking everywhere for you. We've been to both your homes and to your grandmother's and to Miss What's-her-name, the woman who owns that dog." Alice looked at a notebook in her hand. "Miss Finucane's."

"We've been here most of the morning," the Professor said.

"Talking to your friends while there are things to be done. And we've lost the photographers."

"What photographers?" asked Spike.

"The ones who are going to take your photographs, of course. There should be people from the television as well but that crazy driver of ours just would not slow down."

"That's because you were telling him to go fast," said Martin Daly. Then he straightened his tie slightly and grinned. "What do you think of the get-up?"

"It's great," said Spike.

"Brand new, every stitch, from top to toe. Four attendants dancing around me in the finest shop in Dublin."

"Well, we couldn't have you going around in the clothes you wore to the races," declared

Alice. "They looked as though you'd slept in them."

"Which I probably had," laughed Martin.

Alice was not amused. "No jokes, please," she said. "This is a very serious matter." She stared at Spike and the Professor. Then at Doreen and Brunhilde. "Where did you get that frock?" she asked Brunhilde.

"It was a present from..."

But Alice's attention was now on a Transit van that had pulled in behind the long black car. "There they are, at long last. You," and she pointed at Winky, "what's your name?"

"Winky," said Winky.

For a second, it seemed as though Alice thought this was another joke, but then decided she did not have the time to go into the matter. "All right, Winky. Go and tell the people in the van to come over here."

The people in the van proved to be a group of cross-looking reporters and photographers, who had spent the last half-hour hurtling around Sandymount and Irishtown far too fast for their idea of safety and comfort.

They glared at Winky and then at Alice.

Alice said "This is your chance to get some authentic pictures of the young people lucky enough to have been invited to London by

Jenny South and Daly Carson."

"I thought you worked for The Tree-Tops,"
Spike said as Alice started to push Winky and
his crowd out of the way.

"So I do, but I had to stay in Dublin to
attend to one or two things so Jenny and Daly
asked me if I would look after all of you as
well."

"Are The Tree-Tops still in Dublin then?"
asked the Professor.

"What? Oh yes, or at least...Oh for heaven's
sake, why does everyone have to start asked
me questions that I don't know the..." She
stopped herself just in time from finishing the
sentence but it was perfectly clear to Spike
and the Professor that if she had finished it, it
would have been with the words "answers to."

The two boys exchanged amazed glances.
How could Alice Hopper not know where The
Tree-Tops were? Then they both remembered
that she had lost them before the races and
had mistaken Spike and the Professor for
them.

As if to prevent them from continuing the
conversation, Alice began to push them
around as well, patting at their hair, straight-
ening their collars while yelling at Winky and
company to get further out of the way.

"I'm not moving," declared Imelda Flood.

But it was as though Alice hadn't heard her. She just took the bouzouki away from her and handed it to Spike. "Look as though you are playing it," she ordered.

"I'm the musician," Brunhilde said.

The television crew had arrived by now. There were five people: a thin pale director who kept flapping his hands around, a thin pale cameraman who kept moving his camera around, a thin pale soundman who kept trying to find out what to do with the microphones, a pale young woman with a notebook and a very pretty, curly-haired woman, whom all the young people recognised at once.

"It's Meg Oatfield," Imelda said in an awed voice.

Meg waved. The director said, "Sorry. We got lost."

"Not to worry," Alice said, faking a relaxed smile. "The press haven't finished with them yet."

For the next few minutes, our four leading characters had to stand this way and that way, to look up and to look down, to smile, to be serious, to pretend to be listening to Spike playing the bouzouki. Then Brunhilde insisted that she be allowed to really play it. The music she made sounded very strange but that didn't worry Brunhilde. She was in her element.

Alice took over once more when the reporters began to ask questions. No matter whom the question was directed at, Alice always provided the answer.

"Yes, the young people were looking forward to going to London."

"Yes, Jenny and Daly were planning to give them a terrific time."

"Of course, they will all go to the Tree-Tops' concert."

"Of course, everyone is delighted with everyone."

While all this was going on, Spike sidled up to Martin Daly. "Why aren't you in any of the photographs?"

"Oh they took ones of me earlier on."

"Have you seen The Tree-Tops since Saturday?"

"Funny you should ask that," Martin replied. "There's some kind of a mystery there. I heard Alice on the phone and I got the impression that, for some reason or another, she's very worried about Scarce and the Mole and Speedy."

"The Professor is supposed to be like the Mole and I'm supposed to be like Speedy."

"You don't look a bit like them now then but, of course, that's maybe because you're all washed and in nice clean clothes. But that Brunhilde would pass for a film star any hour of the day or night."

Spike looked at Brunhilde and, for the first time, noticed what she was actually wearing. It was a long, beige-coloured dress with a deep fringe at the hemline and equally deep fringes at the ends of the sleeves.

As the reporters and photographers went back to the van, followed by Alice busily answering questions that no-one was asking, Brunhilde was turning her attention to the TV crew. "If I'd realised that you were coming, I'd have worn something a bit more colourful. I could slip back to the O'Neills' and change."

"We haven't time for that," the director said, "not if we are going to get this finished for this evening's programme."

Brunhilde looked cross. Meg Oatfield said soothingly, "It's a lovely dress. What's it made of?"

"Deerskin," Brunhilde said.

Meg looked shocked. "Real deerskin?"

"Oh yes, but the skin of a deer that was killed a long time ago for its meat. I couldn't possibly wear a frock made of the skin of an animal that had been killed just for its skin.

Heavens, no!"

Meg looked relieved. "Was it your father who killed the deer?"

Brunhilde laughed. "Heavens, no! He and Mom don't know one end of a rifle from another. The deer was killed by the ancestors of the old Indian who taught my parents the dance of greeting to the sun."

Brunhilde's voice was having its usual effect. Even Imelda seemed to have forgotten her determination to get her bouzouki back.

"My parents and I perform the dance every morning. I could perform it for you now if you like. In fact, what really might be interesting would be if I were to teach it to some Irish people as a kind of 'thank-you' for the way they've treated me."

Imelda and Winky and his gang were as putty in her hands when she turned her blue eyes on them. "These folks here, for example, might feel better if they started the day with a dance. It could make them understand things better. It would look mighty interesting on TV as well."

The cameraman and the soundman nodded in agreement. So too did Winky and his friends, suddenly delighted to find that Brunhilde had not only decided to forgive and forget the harsh words that had passed between them, but was actually going to include them in the TV programme.

The pale young woman was quickly making notes of what Brunhilde was saying.

"Don't worry," Brunhilde said. "We can record the interview after we've done the number."

She's carrying on as though she's directing a Hollywood musical, thought Spike.

"Follow me," Brunhilde said to the young people.

All of them, with the exception of Spike, the Professor and Doreen, followed Brunhilde down on to the strand. "Line up now in three rows!" She smiled at Imelda. "Is it all right if I use your bouzouki to play the rhythm?"

Imelda nodded.

"Good. Why don't you come to the middle of the front row where you can be seen? After all, if you hadn't thought to bring the bouzouki, how could we have managed?"

Imelda took the place indicated to her.

"Now, after I count to three," Brunhilde said, "you lift your left foot. Then your right foot, only follow the beat." She began to thump the back of the bouzouki. "Left foot! Right foot! Turn in a circle like this! Put a bit of meaning into it! You are greeting the sun, not peeling an orange!"

The Professor nodded at Spike. Brandy, who had taken refuge under the seat as soon as Alice started to order everyone around, slipped out and followed the two boys away from the tower.

The only person to notice them leaving was Doreen who, after watching the TV crew getting ready to record the dance to the rising sun, ran after them.

"Where are you going?"

"We thought Brandy deserved a proper walk before the day gets too hot. He's been very patient," the Professor said.

"And, anyway, we'd had enough of Brunhilde's carry-on," said Spike.

"Brunhilde doesn't mean any harm." Doreen felt it was her duty to defend her new friend although she was inclined to agree with her brother.

"No, but she causes harm all the same. Just look back there now. It was all lovely and peaceful until about fifteen minutes ago."

Spike was right. The situation had changed beyond recognition as drivers slowed down to gape at what looked like a fair-haired Indian encouraging a group of twelve-year-olds to prepare for tribal warfare. Toddlers were seized by anxious mothers and strapped into buggies. Practising golfers ceased to address the ball. The sea-birds left their feeding-grounds and flew to the safety of the lighthouse wall.

"At least, we know now that we are definitely going to London, so Winky and Imelda can't go on saying we were making it up just to attract attention," said Doreen.

"That is if our parents have agreed," said the Professor. "I know that my mam wasn't all that keen on the idea."

"You never mentioned that until now," said Spike.

"Well, she was a bit tired after the disco." What he really meant, but didn't like to say, was that both his parents seemed to be tired of the Brisks and especially of Brunhilde who had been going on and on and on non-stop about The Tree-Tops and London. He just hoped that Alice Hopper hadn't made things worse when she'd called around looking for him.

"Maybe we should go and talk to her," Doreen said. "Then we could go to our house in Irishtown."

"What about Brunhilde?" asked Spike.

"Oh, she'll be all right," Doreen said, ruefully avoiding her brother's eyes.

"I meant, will it be like this in London? Will she be forever taking charge?"

"We just won't let her," replied the Professor. "We will decide for ourselves what to do. There will be all that sight-seeing."

"She'll be too busy running after The Tree-Tops to do anything as ordinary as sight-seeing," said Doreen.

"That is if The Tree-Tops are there," said Spike.

"But if they aren't in London, where would they be?" asked Doreen.

"That is the question of the day, it seems to me," replied Spike. "You see, I don't think Alice Hopper is at all sure where they are."

"But how can you lose a pop-group a few days before their big concert?" asked Doreen.

"I don't know," said the Professor, "but don't say anything to Brunhilde. Or to our parents about it. They might get into a state and refuse to let us go to London in case we vanished too!"

3
Talking with the Grown-Ups

rs O'Neill was out on the patio, reading a book that she had to review for a newspaper. "Oh, it's you," she said when she saw Brandy and his three companions. "That publicity woman was here looking for you."

"I know. We met her," the Professor said. "We all had our photographs taken near the Tower. Brunhilde is on the strand teaching the others the dance to the rising sun."

"What others?"

"Oh, just some kids from Irishtown."

Mrs O'Neill seemed far from pleased to hear this. "If you ask me, this whole business is getting out of hand."

"Do you mean the trip to London when you say that?" asked Doreen.

"That and other things that have been happening lately. What do your father and mother have to say?"

"Well, not much," Doreen said.

Mrs O'Neill put down her book and studied the young people. "In other words, you have come to try and get me on your side before you talk to them. Well, maybe it's a good time to talk while we have the place to ourselves."

"Are Brunhilde's parents out then?" asked the Professor.

"Yes, with your father. He's taken them for a drive. They've hardly seen the city."

"Did *they* say anything about London?" asked Doreen.

"They hardly needed to. Brunhilde has them brainwashed. I think they'd let her go even if we never heard from Daly and Jenny again." Mrs O'Neill smiled when she said "Daly". He was, to her, one of the most charming, handsome men in the world. "But, if the invitation did come through, we'd have to decide who'd be in charge of you."

"The invitation has come through. That's why Brunhilde is giving dance lessons. The TV people are recording it," said the Professor. "And the invitation included everyone. You and Dad and Mrs and Mrs O'Halligan and the

Brisks and Granny O'Brien and Mrs Hurt and her grandson, Wally..."

"And Martin Daly," added Doreen, "So there would be plenty of people to keep an eye on us."

"And there are two houses," said Spike. "Daly is renting one. Jenny is renting the other."

"Even so, we can't all just go off like that," said Mrs O'Neill. 'Your dad has his work to attend to. So, too, in a way, has Damien's".

Doreen sensed it was time to be as direct as possible. She said, "If there is no chance of us being let go, then I think you should tell us now, Mrs O'Neill, so that we can give up the idea once and for all."

Mrs O'Neill was impressed with Doreen's frankness. She said, "All right. I'll try and be as honest with you as you have been with me. We all had a good time at the disco party on Saturday night. It was great meeting all those famous people but we don't belong in their world. I am worried in case it might be too unsettling for you to go and stay with them in London."

"But it's only for the weekend," said the Professor. "We'll be out sightseeing most of the time. We know that when the weekend is over we will come back here and live the way we always have. We aren't expecting anything marvellous to happen."

"Brunhilde is," said Spike.

"Brunhilde always expects that," said the Professor. "But I'm sure, once we get to London, that she'll realise that Scarce was only being polite when he said he'd listen to her songs."

"So you see, you've no need to worry about us getting swelled heads or anything like that," said Doreen. "Would Granny O'Brien be all right to look after us?"

"It hardly seems fair to a woman of her years to give her that responsibility," said Mrs O'Neill.

"What if Wally was to come with us? You met him on Saturday. He organised the party."

"I must say he struck me as being very intelligent," said Mrs O'Neill.

"He's going to be a doctor," said Spike.

"And he's only nineteen so he'd be well able to go around with us," said the Professor.

Mrs O'Neill sighed. "It really means that much to you? And why wouldn't it? If the chance of such a trip had come my way when I was your age, I'd have been delighted as well."

"Are you saying 'yes' then?" asked the Professor.

"On condition that Mr and Mrs O'Halligan agree and that we are all satisfied with the arrangements. Also on condition that Wally goes with you. Also on condition..."

But, whatever the final condition was, it went unheard by the three young people as they dashed out of the back garden with Brandy back on his lead.

"Where first?" asked the Professor.

"Granny O'Brien," said Spike. "Then to see our Mam. Dad'll agree with what she decides. Then to Martin Daly to find out what time the plane goes." He started down the road.

"You're going in the wrong direction," said Doreen.

"No, I'm not. There's a bus coming. We'll take it to Irishtown. That way we won't risk meeting Brunhilde."

The trio ran upstairs to the top of the bus. Brandy had never been on a bus before and didn't care for the way the floor trembled so he jumped up on the Professor's lap and looked out the window, delighted, now that he felt comfortable, to get a completely new look at the world. Coming back down the stairs was tricky but, once on the pavement, he felt even better. Granny O'Brien was, as always, pleased to see him and let him lie in the cool hall of her house while she listened to what her two grandchildren and the Professor had to say.

She then made a telephone call. Although her visitors could only hear one side of the conversation, they felt that everything was going fine. This was confirmed when she came back and declared that both Mrs Hurt and Wally were all in favour of the trip to London.

"Now for Mam," said Doreen as the trio and dog hurried towards the O'Halligan house.

Mrs Moody, newspaper in hand, scowled at them as they ran by her.

"Doesn't that woman ever stay at home?" asked the Professor.

"Who cares?" replied Spike. "Now, Brandy, we want you to lie down here on the pavement and not move. Understood?"

Brandy lay down and put his front paws over his ears. That way he hoped to shut out the sound of any insulting remarks from a certain terrier who lived around the corner and thought he owned the world.

He had not to wait very long before the trio came back out and did what looked like a quieter version of Brunhilde's dance. Obviously Mrs O'Halligan had given her blessing to the London trip.

"Now for Martin Daly," said Spike. "I know the house he lives in."

They hurried past the red-brick school that

the two boys attended. It looked strange and silent in the bright sunshine. At this hour, during term-time, the yard would be thronged with boys.

The Star of the Sea Church was equally quiet, waiting for people to arrive for ten o'clock mass.

"That's the house there," said Spike. "He's bound to have gone back there after watching Brunhilde's carry-on."

But none of the three bells on the door had Martin's name on it. "Of course, he said he borrowed the flat," Doreen remembered. "He's on the top floor, Maybe we should ring the top bell."

They rang the top bell. Nothing happened.

They rang the middle bell. Nothing happened.

They rang the bottom bell. A busy-looking woman opened the door. "What do you want?"

"We're looking for Mr Daly," Doreen said.

"He doesn't live here any more. He's gone to the Granville." Seeing the blank look on the young people's faces, she added, "That's the big new hotel in the middle of the city. He's supposed to be the long-lost cousin of someone famous."

"He's Daly Carson's cousin," said Doreen. "Daly Carson of *The Huntingtons of Hunting-*

ton Hall."

The woman said, "I never cared much for him: too many teeth." Then she closed the door.

Doreen said, "We can't bring Brandy to the Granville. They wouldn't let him in. We'll have to take him back to Miss Finucane's."

"And here's another bus," said Spike.

Brandy couldn't believe his luck; two bus-rides in one day! A pity, though, that it meant less of a walk for him. An even greater pity was that, when they got off the bus at the stop beyond the tower, Brunhilde, who had finally called an end to the dance lesson, saw them. "Wait," she yelled. "Wait for me." To her pupils, all of whom were gasping for breath, she said, "Right. I want you all back here at nine in the morning. Anyone who is late will not appear in the show."

"What show?" Imelda asked as she took back her bouzouki.

"Why, the Brunhilde Brisk show, of course," said Brunhilde. "As soon as I get back from London, we will really start to work on it." She clambered over the rocks. "Hey, where did you go to?"

"To get our parents' permission to go to London," the Professor said.

"You didn't think they'd say no, did you?"

Brunhilde laughed her great loud laugh. Brandy's tail drooped at the sound. "Why don't you get rid of the mutt and we can talk clothes?"

"Clothes?" said the Professor. "I thought you sorted all that out on Sunday afternoon."

"That was before I appeared on TV," said Brunhilde.

"We're fine as we are," said Spike.

"Oh fiddle-de-dee," said Brunhilde. Then seeing that she was failing to get her own way, she tossed her head and said, "Well, I'm going to make quite sure that I make a good impression. See you later on!"

The others waited until she was out of earshot before speaking. "She'll be furious that we didn't take her with us to the Granville," said Doreen.

"Oh fiddle-de-dee," said Spike, tossing *his* head. "See if I care!"

4
At the Hotel

orty minutes later the trio was standing outside the Granville Hotel.

"It's very posh and expensive looking," said the Professor, realising that his jeans had, in some mysterious way, become creased and covered in dust. Spike looked equally untidy. The piece of hair, which until then had been flat, suddenly stood up on the back of his head.

Even Doreen, who usually managed to stay tidier much longer than the boys, wished she had a mirror handy to see that her face was clean. She almost wished, for a moment, that Brunhilde was with them. Brunhilde would not have been nervous going into what was, after all, just a hotel. Well neither, decided Doreen, would she be nervous.

"Come on," she said and led the way through

the swing doors.

The hotel entrance hall was covered in a thick dark-blue carpet. The reception desk was like an island of light floating on top of it. Young women were working computers and smiling at the guests checking in and out. Opposite the reception desk was the porters' desk, behind which three solemn men, dressed in striped waistcoats and maroon trousers, dealt quickly and efficiently with people's enquiries about theatres and restaurants and shops. When they saw Doreen and her two companions emerge from the swing doors, their expressions changed slightly.

Doreen squared her shoulders and marched up to the reception desk. "We'd like to see Mr Martin Daly," she said.

"Just one second. I'll see which room he is in." But even as the receptionist clicked the computer, Alice Hopper swooped on them. "Oh, so there you are at long last..." Then her words trailed away in a disappointed sigh. "Oh, it's you two, is it?"

She thought we were the Mole and Speedy, realised the Professor, which would also explain the reaction of the three porters. He and Spike must look grubbier than he thought if they could be so easily mistaken for The Tree-

Tops!

Quickly Alice tried to cover up her mistake. "Why did the three of you sneak off when the TV crew started to record the dance?"

"Brunhilde was fine by herself," Doreen said. "We heard that Martin Daly was staying here. We thought he might know about the travel arrangements to London. Have you seen him?"

"He's in there in the lounge. He has a typed copy of the arrangements. I was going to drop copies in at your houses but it slipped my mind."

"Give them to us now, then," said the Professor.

"They're in my room and I don't have time to go back up for them. Get Martin's pages and ask the receptionist to photostat them for you." She glanced at the young woman. "There will be no problem about that, will there?"

"Of course not, Miss Hopper. Our pleasure to help."

"I'll see you all later, then. Be here at two o'clock sharp. Bring Brunhilde with you." Alice swept out through the swing doors and into a taxi.

"She's in a terrible hurry," said Doreen.

"Miss Hopper is always in a hurry," said the receptionist. "But tell me, aren't you the young

people who were involved in all that excitement at the Curragh last Saturday?"

"Yes, we are," Doreen said modestly. "My
brother and his friend here got mistaken for
two of The Tree-Tops."

"Yes, they look very like the two that aren't
very tall for their age."

"Did The Tree-Tops stay here?" asked the
Professor.

"They still are staying here in a kind of a
way."

"How do you mean, 'in a kind of a way'?"

"Well, they never actually checked out,
although I haven't seen them for the last two
days."

"Could they be in their rooms now?" asked
Doreen.

"I don't know but you could try dialling
them on the house phone over there. I assume
you know them well enough for me to give you
the number of their suite?"

"Oh yes," said Doreen, blushing slightly at
the thought that she sounded very like
Brunhilde. "The Tree-Tops are very close, very
dear, very personal friends of ours. We will all
be in London together."

"Then it's Suite 14. Just pick up the phone and
dial that number."

Doreen did as the young woman suggested but no-one answered the phone in Suite 14. "Let's go and get the list from Martin," Spike said. "We can try the number again later on."

The main lounge of the hotel was furnished with sofas and armchairs and low tables. It looked like a huge drawing-room in some great country house. Martin was seated on the biggest of the sofas. On the table in front of him were plates of cakes and sandwiches and a huge pot of tea. He beckoned to the three young people to join him. "Sit down and have a cup of tea. We need more cups, please," he said to a passing waiter.

"Right away, Mr Daly," the waiter replied, bowing slightly.

Martin chuckled with delight. "Did you hear that? Anything I want, I only have to raise my hand and it's brought to me. I never thought the good life was so easy to get used to!"

"My mother is afraid we might get used to it as well," said the Professor.

"And she's right," said Martin, biting into a smoked-salmon sandwich. "People of your age need to learn to fend for themselves. Time enough to take things easy when you get to my time of life!"

"Will you be going to live in America with

your cousin, Daly Carson?" asked Doreen.

"I'm considering the idea," said Martin. "I'm just not sure how lying by a swimming pool in Hollywood will suit me. I've never been one for just lazing about." He finished the smoked-salmon sandwich and took another. "I suppose I could always go into the acting business myself. After all, it runs in the family."

Cripes, that's all we need, thought Spike. Old Martin fancying himself as an actor and Brunhilde thinking she can be a pop-star!

The waiter returned with extra cups and saucers and plates and a fresh pot of tea. "Is there anything else you need, Mr Daly?"

"A few more of those smoked-salmon sandwiches wouldn't go amiss," said Martin.

"Yes, of course, Mr Daly." The waiter bowed slightly again and went away.

"Don't be shy. Tuck in," Martin said, pointing to the sandwiches and the cakes.

As well as smoked salmon, there were chicken sandwiches and tomato squares. "These are lovely," said Doreen, "but we mustn't waste too much time. Have you the list about the travel arrangements that Alice Hopper gave you?"

"I do. It's right here." Martin took the list from his inside pocket.

Doreen and the boys read it quickly. They

were due to leave on the first flight on Friday
morning and come back on the last one on
Monday evening. "We'll have four whole days
there," said Doreen. "We can really get to explore
the city. As soon as we have this list copied, we
must telephone Granny O'Brien and let Mrs
Hurt down in Co. Kildare know as well."

"Do it upstairs in the comfort of my sitting-
room. The calls all go on the bill," suggested
Martin.

"Well, if you're sure that will be all right."

"Of course it will be all right. Ah, now here
are the other sandwiches. Thank you, my good
man."

The waiter placed the second plate of sandwiches on the table and once more went away.

"Maybe we should make the phone calls
now," said the Professor. "Alice Hopper wants
us to be back here at two o'clock. It's half-past
eleven now. We have to get home to our
lunch."

"Have your lunch here," said Martin.

"No, we'd better not, thank you all the
same, Mr Daly," Doreen said. "Our parents
might think that we were being spoiled."

"And if we eat too much now, we won't have
any appetite for what's at home," said Spike.
"Mam might decide that we were getting too

excited over the trip, especially in all this heat."

"Does that mean you won't have another sandwich?" asked Martin.

"Well, maybe, just one more," said Spike.

Doreen and the Professor agreed with this decision.

Five minutes later, not only were all the sandwiches gone but all the cakes too. "Maybe being famous makes you extra hungry," said Spike.

"Well it's certainly given me a fine appetite," said Martin. "I haven't eaten so much in years. Now for the phone calls."

Doreen left the list to be copied at reception and got into the lift with the others. When they got out on the top floor, Martin led the way down the corridor. "They had the whole floor between them," he said proudly. "Jenny South had that suite. Daly had this one here and kept it on just for me. Across the way there is Suite 14 where The Tree-Tops are."

The door to Suite 14 was slightly ajar.

"Do you think it would be all right for us to have a look inside?" asked Doreen.

"I don't see why not, but I thought you were in a terrible hurry."

"It'll only take a few seconds." Doreen knocked several times on the open door before she and the boys entered Suite 14. There were clothes and records and cups and plates scattered all over the place. The bedrooms were just as untidy.

"It's a wonder no-one cleans the place," said the Professor.

"Perhaps they did but it just got untidied again," said Spike. The same thing often happened to his bedroom but never as badly as this.

"At least we know they haven't left Dublin," said Doreen, "although you'd think they would have to if they've to get ready for the big concert in London next Saturday. Anyway, we'd better get out of here."

The suite that Daly was renting for Martin was huge and as tidy as the Tree-Tops' was a mess. Martin pointed to a gold-plated phone on a glass table. "Just press 0 and then dial the number you want."

The first call went to Granny O'Brien, who was as thrilled as the young people over the travel arrangements. Martin insisted on talking to her as well and invited her to dinner at the hotel that evening. "I'll have to see," Granny O'Brien said. "It's just possible that my friend, Mrs Hurt, will come to Dublin to buy a few things when I give her the news."

"She can come to dinner too," said Martin.

"And that big galoot of a grandson of hers. What's his name?"

"Wally Fever," said Granny O'Brien.

"Bedad," said Martin, "what with Wally Fever and Winky Moran, I feel as though I'm in the films already."

"What do you mean 'in the films'?" asked Granny O`Brien.

"Come to dinner this evening and I'll tell you all."

"I'll let you know for sure this afternoon," said Granny O`Brien.

"If I'm not here, leave a message at reception," Martin said. Then he replaced the receiver and roared with laughter. "And to think that this time last week, I was up to my ears in debt! Now, who else do you need to phone?"

"No-one. Granny will talk to Mrs Hurt. We can tell our own parents when we get home," said Doreen, "only we'd better hurry."

"I can send you home in a taxi if you like."

"No, thank you all the same, Mr Daly. We'll be fine."

The young people arrived home in perfect time for lunch. Granny O'Brien was in the O'Halligan house, having just slipped around to discuss the arrangements with her daughter, Mrs O'Halligan, so there was no problem for

Spike and Doreen there.

Brunhilde, although thrilled to learn that everything was going so well, was very cross to have missed the visit to the hotel.

"You could have come with us if you wanted to," the Professor said patiently. "But you'll be seeing it this afternoon when we meet Alice. I wonder what she wants us for now. She rushed off before we had a chance to ask."

"And before you rush off out of here," said Mrs O'Neill, "you are going upstairs to have a good wash and change into your flannels and a clean shirt. No arguments, please! You are a positive disgrace!"

"Do you think I should change as well?" asked Brunhilde. "This dress is all right for giving dance lessons in but it might not suit a smart hotel."

"Whatever you think best," Mrs O'Neill said.

"I'll change," said Brunhilde.

As soon as she left the kitchen, Mrs O'Neill said to her son, "Do you know anything about the Brunhilde Brisk show?"

"No," said the Professor, truthfully.

The same question was being asked in the O'Halligan household by Mrs O'Halligan. "Several women that I know stopped me on my way to do the shopping and asked me what exactly was involved in being part of the Brunhilde Brisk show. You're sure that you two aren't mixed up in it?"

Doreen and Spike nodded.

"Try and keep it that way then," said Mrs O'Halligan. "I don't want parents around here complaining any more than you want more trouble with Winky and Imelda and their mates. Now you are to wash and change before you meet Alice Hopper. And remember you are not to agree to anything until you talk it over with me and your Dad."

Alice Hopper was furious when she heard what Mrs O'Halligan had said. "How can I possibly arrange things if I have to keep going back to all your mothers to get their approval?"

"There are only two mothers and two fathers, ours and his," Spike said, nodding at the Professor.

"I have a Dad and a Mom as well," Brunhilde reminded him.

"Yes, but they let you do anything that you want."

"That's because they know they can trust me." Brunhilde glanced at herself in the mirrored wall of the lounge. She was wearing a large black hat with red ribbons down the back, a bright pink blouse and chocolate-coloured jeans tucked into dark brown boots.

Spike thought she looked like a jam roll that had been left too long in the oven.

Doreen wished she could pick and choose her clothes like Brunhilde. Alice thought Brunhilde had gone far too far with the outfit that she was wearing. And said so.

"You show no dress sense at all," she said. "We are going straight from here to a very up-to-date store where they will supply you with all the latest fashions."

"But who's going to pay for them?" asked the Professor.

"It's an arrangement I have with them."

"What sort of arrangement?" demanded Doreen, remembering her promise to consult her mother before agreeing to anything.

"In return for a certain amount of publicity, they give us certain clothes for nothing. They just want you to be photographed in them."

"I don't think our Mam would like that very much," said Spike. "It'd look like we were too poor to buy our own things."

"And my mother would think it was going to make us too used to attention if we started being treated like fashion models," said the Professor. "And, anyway, I don't think I want to be a model."

"Oh don't be so dull," said Brunhilde. "What's a few more photographs, for heaven's sake? Leave it all to me, honey," she said to Alice. "I'll soon fix things. Where is there a telephone that I can use?"

The receptionist, who had photostated the list of travel arrangements earlier in the day and who had been listening with great interest to the conversation between Alice and the young people, said, "You can use the telephone here, if you like."

"Terrific," said Brunhilde. "Now I need your Mom's number and also that of the O'Halligan household."

Very reluctantly, the Professor wrote down his number. With equal reluctance, Doreen called out the telephone number for the house in Irishtown.

When Mrs O'Neill answered Brunhilde said, "Hi there, Mrs O'Neill. We are all in the Granville Hotel with Alice Hopper and guess what she has managed to arrange for us? A whole new wardrobe each..." A frown appeared as Brunhilde listened to Mrs O'Neill's reaction. Then the frown vanished and she laughed. She said, "Gracious, no, I didn't mean that we were each getting a piece of furniture. I meant we were all to be given a whole lot of free clothes."

She listened again to Mrs O'Neill. Then she said, "No, all we need to do is to have some photos taken. Isn't it terrific? Aren't you proud?"

Obviously Mrs O'Neill was not as proud as Brunhilde had hoped and asked to speak to Alice.

Alice said, "Yes, Mrs O'Neill, this is Alice Hopper. I hope you are not going to make difficulties over a simple matter of free clothing."

The Professor groaned. That was quite the worst way to speak to his mother when she was not in the best of humours. Alice turned bright red at whatever Mrs O'Neill said and then silently handed the phone to the Professor.

Mrs O'Neill said, in a voice that would freeze rain drops in the Sahara, "Damien, the clothes that you already have are more than adequate for this trip to London. Is that understood?"

"Yes, Mam."

"If you should need more, we will buy them for you. Is that understood?"

"Yes, Mam."

"I'll expect you home by five o'clock for tea. Is that understood?"

"Yes, Mam."

"Good. Now good-bye."

"She said *no*?" exclaimed Brunhilde in disbelief. "She actually said no! Well, I hope Doreen's mother has more sense."

She dialled the O'Halligan number. It was engaged.

"That means that my mother is speaking to Mrs O'Halligan," said the Professor. "She's telling her what she just told us."

"Which means it's no as far as we are concerned too," said Spike.

"Well, I'm certainly not saying no to such a good offer," said Brunhilde. "Doreen, you can help me choose things. Where exactly is the shop?"

"I'm not sure if they'll be bothered just with one of you?" said Alice.

"Of course they will, especially when they realise that I am going to be so famous in just a matter of weeks."

"Well, all right. We can but try," said Alice, realising that not even she could stand up to Brunhilde when Brunhilde was being so determined.

"Can the boys come along too?" asked Doreen.

"No. We'll go and see Martin," Spike said. "We'll see you later on."

"Suit yourselves," Alice said.

"Hey, that's a real good joke, seeing as how they aren't allowed to accept any free clothes," laughed Brunhilde as she led Doreen and Alice to the swing doors.

The boys looked in the lounge. Martin wasn't there. They went up in the lift and knocked on the door of his suite. He wasn't there either.

They looked across the corridor at the door of Suite 14. "He might be in there," Spike said. Both he and the Professor knew that they really wanted an excuse to see if there was any sign of The Tree-Tops.

But even as they moved to knock at the door of Suite 14, that door was opened by a heavy-set man with greying hair and dark brown eyes. "So you're back, are you?" he snarled.

"Back?" said Spike.

The man stepped towards them. "Don't get clever with me!"

At that moment, the lift doors opened again. A porter, carrying suitcases, led a man and a woman down the corridor towards the suite where Jenny South had stayed.

The porter smiled at the man and the two boys. "You've found them, I see. At least, I think you have."

The man stared hard at Spike and the Professor again. Then, with a growl of rage, he hurried to the lift and got into it just as the doors closed.

The porter and the couple moved on. The woman laughed as the porter explained what had happened. The boys realised that the man who had come out of Suite 14 had thought they were the Mole and Speedy. For a second they thought of trying to catch up with him. But then they decided that, before they rushed into anything and ended up in fresh trouble, they should bide their time and try to find out, nice and quietly, what exactly was going on.

At the clothes shop Brunhilde ignored all advice offered by Alice and Doreen. She kept trying on half of one outfit with half of another. The shop manager finally said, "This is ridiculous! She may choose one outfit and one outfit only! There will be no need to photograph her in it! Just take her away from here!"

These remarks made Brunhilde so cross that she said she would wear nothing from the shop and flounced off! So in a way everybody was suited and no trouble was caused with any of the parents.

5
Taking Off

ally drove Mrs Hurt, Mrs O'Brien, Spike and Doreen to the airport and left his car in the long-term car-park.

The real Professor, since he was just dropping Brunhilde and his son off, used the short-term car-park where they found a trolley to take the luggage.

"There's Alice Hopper!" Brunhilde said as soon as they came into the main terminal. "Oooo, over here!"

"Oh good, you're here." Alice glanced anxiously at her watch.

"If you're in a hurry, there's no need for you to wait," the real Professor said.

Alice managed to smile. "Well, it would suit me to get back into the city."

"You're not coming with us, then?" said Wally.

"No. I have some business to attend to..."

"At this time of the day?" asked Granny O'Brien.

"Yes, but I hope to catch a plane later in the afternoon. Your tickets are all here in this envelope. Who's going to take charge of them?"

"Wally," everyone else said.

"Oh, right. Now if you're sure you don't need me for anything else..." Alice again looked at her watch.

"No. We'll be fine," Wally said.

"She's always in such a hurry," Mrs Hurt said, as Alice made for the exit. "When we had dinner with Martin in the hotel, she was in and out of the place like an electrified chicken all evening long. By the way, where is Martin?"

"He's right here," replied the man in question, pushing his way through the crowd. He was unshaven and looked cross.

"What happened to you?" asked Granny O'Brien.

"It's more a question of what happened to Alice Hopper," Martin replied. "She was supposed to arrange to have me called but didn't. If I hadn't happened to wake up I'd still be sound asleep in my bed. I'd never have been in time for the flight."

"Excuse me. Are you the Carson South group?"

The question was asked by a young woman dressed in a smart green uniform.

"Yes, we are," Wally smiled eagerly.

"Oh good. I'm Claire Redmond. I've just come along to see that everything is all right. May I see your tickets, please?"

Wally handed her the envelope. "Ah yes, of course, you are travelling Executive Class," she said. " Just follow me, please." She looked back at Martin. " Have you no luggage?"

"Luggage?" A new expression of dismay settled on Martin's face. "I left the hotel in such a hurry that I clean forgot to pack a single thing. All my grand new clothes are in the bedroom at the Granville!"

"Alice Hopper could bring them with her," Doreen suggested. "She was hoping to be on an afternoon flight."

"They will have the number of the hotel at the information desk. Just ask them to dial it for you," Claire said.

"It'll also give you the perfect excuse to enquire about any messages for you," Spike whispered. "Will the Professor and I come with you?"

"No. That'll just bring Brunhilde back snooping. I'll come over to you when I've finished," Martin replied.

The check-in took less than three minutes.
Seats had already been reserved for them so
that they could sit together. "Now, there is a
special lounge if you care to wait there," Claire
said. "You could have some tea or coffee".

Brunhilde said, "We'll wait for breakfast on
the plane."

"Speak for yourself, young lady," Mrs Hurt
said. " I wouldn't mind a cup of tea right now.
And why do you keep bobbing up and down
like that?"

"I was just looking around."

"Looking around for what?"

"For her friends, The Tree-Tops," Wally suggested, "or maybe a few reporters and photographers."

"Sure you've got more publicity out of it all
than the jockey who rode the winner in the big
race on Saturday," declared Mrs Hurt.

"Oh and talking of winners, we never got
our share of the winnings from Daly Carson,"
Spike said. "It's as well we have some money
of our own."

"Well now, as it so happens, I have your
racing money here," said Granny O'Brien
"And you'll get it as soon as we arrive in London. And here's Martin back."

"What did they say at the hotel?" Wally

asked as he handed Martin his boarding card.

"Oh, they'll pack my stuff and give it to Alice to take to London."

"And what about the message to wake you?" asked Spike.

"Alice Hopper telephoned minutes after I drove off in the taxi."

"She must have telephoned from here," the Professor said.

Brunhilde stared at Doreen and the two boys. "There is definitely something going on."

"Is this true, Doreen? Spike?" Granny O'Brien enquired in a stern voice.

"We're not sure," Doreen said.

"And until we are sure why cause any upset?" asked Wally, shepherding the two elderly ladies towards the boarding area.

Doreen and Spike smiled gratefully at their saviour. The Professor felt thankful that his father hadn't heard what had been said. The real Professor had dropped his ticket to the car park and was looking for it on the floor. He found it under the foot of a dark, heavy set man. "Excuse me, my car-park ticket—it's under your foot."

"What?" The man turned and looked at the real Professor. Then lifting his foot, he resumed his watching of a particular group of

people. The real Professor realised that it was
Spike and company who were being watched.

Quickly he crossed over to his son. "Do you
know that man over there?"

The other Professor turned and saw no-one
that he recognised. "What man?"

"I just thought that he seemed very interested in you."

Brunhilde smiled, taking it as a compli-
ment. Spike knew that there was more to it than
that. He'd seen the real Professor speak to the
man, and before he disappeared into the crowd,
he had recognised him as the same man who
had come out of Suite 14 at the Granville Hotel.
But he decided to say nothing to the other Professor until Brunhilde was well out of earshot.

Brunhilde gave the real Professor a big hug.
"Thanks for driving us out so early in the day."

The real Professor hugged her back and
almost felt sorry that he was not travelling
with her and his son. "Have a terrific time. You
too, Damien."

The real Professor and the other Professor
hugged each other. Then it seemed as though
everyone else wanted to hug the real Professor
too before they went through security, into the
duty-free shops where Wally bought himself a
portable, voice-activated tape recorder. Brun-

hilde immediately made him promise she
could borrow it when he wasn't using it. Then
Doreen saw some lovely Irish linen table-mats
and it was agreed that they should all chip in
and buy two sets: one for Daly Carson and one
for Jenny South.

They went on board the aircraft almost
immediately, first thanking Claire for all her
help. The young people all had window seats
and, within minutes of fastening their safety
belts, they felt the engines throb into life. Down
the runway they went and then up into the
clear blue sky.

The great curve of Dublin Bay was visible
in all its detail, including the great chimmeys
at the Pigeon House, the strand and the Martello Tower at Sandymount, the traffic on
Strand Road. Even the houses that they knew
could be picked out before the aircraft banked
to the left and the view of the city was replaced
by the sea where an occasional fishing boat
could be seen.

"It's wonderful," Doreen said, "absolutely
wonderful."

"I think I'm going to make a song up about
it," said Brunhilde.

Fortunately, at that moment, the hostesses
began to serve breakfast. Brunhilde kept on

commenting on how delicious it was, almost as though she had been responsible for its preparation. By the time they had finished and the trays were cleared away, they were flying down across England where they could see the pattern of fields and houses and cities and villages and a network of motorways, whose traffic reflected the sunshine, like stones in a shallow stream.

The chief stewardess switched on the microphone and announced that they were now approaching London, Heathrow, and hoped to be landing in a few minutes' time. But first they had to wait their turn and circle the city.

Wally, who had been to London several times before, leaned across Spike and began to identify the buildings. "Those are the Houses of Parliament. You can see Big Ben on top of the tower. And that's Westminster Abbey and the Festival Hall. If you look out the other side, you can see St Paul's Cathedral and those tall buildings are in what's known as "The City," a sort of city within the city where the Bank of England and the Stock Exchange are."

The plane turned back towards Heathrow Airport.

We are here, the Professor thought. We are actually here in London!

6

Regent's Park

he customs hall in Heathrow was even busier than the departure terminal at Dublin, as people milled around, waiting for their luggage. The luggage from the Dublin flight was at last indicated to arrive on Carousel Number Seven. But only two pieces got safely off the conveyor belt before it jammed and an official had to jump up and see what had happened. It was, of course, a huge case belonging to Brunhilde that had caused the blockage.

"What on earth have you got in that?" demanded Martin.

"You'll see soon enough," Brunhilde said with one of her "special" smiles.

As it turned out, she spoke more accurately than she had at first imagined for, as she was wheeling her trolley through the "nothing-to-declare" section of customs control, one of the officers made her open the case.

The contents turned out to be dozens of sheets of words and music, "All my own work," Brunhilde proudly declared as the officer examined them.

Also in the case were at least six pairs of shoes.

"Just in case," Brunhilde told the officer, who did not dare to ask just in case of what?

But the most surprising item in the case was Imelda Flood's bouzouki.

"Borrowed from a friend," Brunhilde said as she repacked the case.

"You never said Imelda had loaned you her bouzouki," Doreen said.

"Oh, didn't I?"

"No, you didn't. Are you sure she knows you borrowed it?"

"I'll send her a postcard explaining. After yesterday's dance lesson, she forgot to take it back. When I realised that I still had it, it seemed a shame not to bring it."

"It could have been smashed, putting it in the case like that."

"Except that it wasn't..."

"Girls, for goodness sake, can't you see you are holding everyone up?" Granny O'Brien said.

Doreen walked quickly out of the customs hall. Her face was very grim. Brunhilde had no right to just take Imelda's bouzouki like that. Imelda was bound to decide that Doreen had known about it, perhaps even think that Doreen had encouraged her. "Trouble, trouble," Doreen muttered to the boys. "Brunhilde is going to cause trouble."

"Look," said Spike. "There's that man again."

The man coming out of the custom shall stopped, surprised as the three young people stared at him. He must have been on the same flight as they were but seated in the economy section, where they couldn't see him. He had obviously waited in the customs hall until he thought they would be well out of sight. Now there was nothing he could do except walk straight past, which he did without looking at them.

Two uniformed chauffeurs held up cards with the words "Daly and O'Neill" on them.

"That's us," Martin said.

"Miss South and Mr Carson apologise for not coming to meet you themselves," the older of the chauffeurs said, "but were sure you would understand."

"Oh sure," said Brunhilde. "They couldn't risk being mobbed by their fans."

"Actually, they are both working today. They

had a very early start at the studio. My name
is Fred. I work for Mr Carson."

"And I'm Ned. I work for Miss South. Perhaps we could sort out the luggage."

"This, this, this and this are mine," Brunhilde pointed to the trolley. "Those are Doreen's. These two belong to Mrs Hurt and Mrs
O'Brien."

"Thank you. The arrangement is that the
ladies will come with me to Miss South's. The
gentlemen will be staying at Mr Carson's. The
houses are next door to each other."

"That sounds dandy," Brunhilde said.

The cars that the chauffeurs drove were the
longest that any of the visitors, with the exception of Brunhilde, had ever seen. "They are
called 'stretch limos'," she explained, "which is
short for limousines long enough for you to be
able to stretch out in."

"Bedad," said Martin as Fred held the door
open for him, "not only could you stretch out in
this one, but you could open a bowling alley in
it as well."

Driving into London was like floating on a
cushion. Martin seemed to have a story to tell
for every district they drove through.

Then they were in a part of the city which
he didn't know with huge houses glimpsed

behind garden walls, trees, football pitches and a strange glass building that seemed to be filled with birds.

"What's that?" asked Martin.

"Part of the zoo," Fred said. "We are in Regent's Park now."

Spike and the Professor thought it looked like the Phoenix Park, but no private house such as the one they were now approaching, would have been found overlooking the Dublin park.

It was enormous with a wrought-iron gate that opened when Fred pressed a button on the car's dashboard. Television cameras set on top of the pillars recorded their arrival. A carefully-raked drive, curving between beds of roses, led to the front door, which was opened, as soon as the car arrived, by Miss Richardson, Daly Carson's secretary.

"Welcome to London. You must be Mr Daly." She and Martin shook hands. "You have no idea how delighted we all are that you and Mr Carson have met."

"It was a great thrill for me as well," Martin said. "This is Wally Fever."

"Hello, Wally. I'm Amanda Richardson. And, of course, these two young men are Spike and the Professor. Mr Carson was so sorry not to be able to meet you. I hope Fred explained?"

"Oh yes, indeed."

"Then, please, let me show you to your rooms."

The inside of the house was even more impressive than the outside. Mirrors and antique furniture shone from every niche. Priceless paintings hung on the walls. Servants in uniform moved silently about, tending to their duties, smiling briefly at the visitors.

Spike and the Professor shared a bedroom with two huge beds in it, its own bathroom and a television set.

Wally's room, next door, was equally luxurious. But most impressive of all was Martin's, which was twice the size of the other two.

"If you're not too tired, I thought we would go next door to Miss South's and make plans for the day," Amanda said.

Jenny South's house was almost exactly the same as Daly Carson's, with a similar security system.

"Do they always live next door to each other?" Spike asked.

"Only when it is convenient," Amanda said, "such as right now. They are filming part of *The Huntingtons of Huntington Hall* here in England. They lead totally separate lives most of the time."

Brunhilde opened the front door. She obviously saw herself as being immediately in charge of things.

"First thing I want to do is to contact The Tree-Tops," she told the others when they had gathered in the drawing room, "especially Scarce."

"Couldn't that wait until Alice Hopper gets here with Martin's luggage?" Wally suggested.

"I'm afraid it will more or less *have* to wait until then," said Peter Arnew, who was Jenny's secretary. "We don't know how to contact The Tree-Tops. Miss South or Mr Carson may have the number. Amanda and I have to go down to the studio later on in the morning. If we get a chance, we can ask them for it."

"I'll come to the studio with you," Brunhilde said.

"Oh, I'm afraid that's not possible. At least, not today," Amanda said. "We thought that you might like to go sightseeing while the weather is fine."

"Gee, I don't know," Brunhilde said.

"It might be your inspiration for some new songs," Wally added. "The Tree-Tops might just be looking for a new song about London."

"That could be true," said Brunhilde.

"We can leave one of the cars with you," Peter

said. "We'll need the other for ourselves."

"I think I might give the sightseeing a miss," said Martin.

"So might myself and Mrs Hurt," said Granny O'Brien. "We have both seen all the famous tourist places. We thought we would just have a nice mooch around, visiting the places we knew as girls, when we worked in London. Some of the people we knew then might actually still be there."

"That's exactly my plan," Martin said. "Why don't the three of us do it together?"

"Take the car," Wally said. "Cause an absolute sensation when you pull up in it!"

"And what about us?" demanded Brunhilde. "Should we not cause a sensation as well?"

"Not until you've felt the pulse of the city," Wally said. "Not until you've seen it as the ordinary person sees it. You must experience travel on the underground, the view from the top of a bus, the hassle and energy on the streets, the feeling of being part of a crowd. Later on, when you are rich and famous, you won't be able to enjoy these things. You will have to live behind high walls with TV cameras to protect you."

Brunhilde considered Wally's words. "I guess maybe you're right."

"Before you go," Spike said to his granny,

"do you think we could have the money that Daly Carson owes us?"

"No doubt that you'll do well in life!" Granny O'Brien said, taking pound notes out of her handbag. "Ten each. You'll have to go to a bank to change them for English money."

"Or keep them until you go back to Dublin," said Peter. "Miss South left these envelopes for you and the two girls."

"And Mr Carson left these."

The two secretaries handed the boys two envelopes. "To be divided between you. And one for Wally from Mr Carson."

"And one for Wally from Miss South."

Wally said, "No, no! I couldn't! I really couldn't!"

But all the same he did, and was delighted that the two stars had been so kind and thoughtful.

On Amanda's advice, they walked across Regent's Park to the tube-station.

"Have we a plan," Brunhilde asked, "of where we are actually going?"

"Let's see first how much money we have to spend," Spike suggested.

The five of them sat on a bench in the shade of drooping trees. Doreen opened Jenny's envelope. Spike opened Daly Carson's. Each envelope contained four twenty-pound notes.

"That's forty pounds each," said Spike. "How much did you get, Wally?"

"Sixty pounds," Wally said.

"It's a small fortune," the Professor said.

"We'll go on a bus tour," Wally said. "That's always the best way to see a new city. They are bound to be able to tell us at the ticket office in the Underground where such tours begin."

7

London Town

heir first experience of the London Underground was unnerving.

The clerk in the ticket office at Regent's Park suggested they go to Piccadilly Circus where they would find buses offering around the city tours.

The train, when it came along, was so crowded that it was sheer luck that they all ended up in the same carriage. Wally, being so tall, was able to see above the heads of the crowd but the others had elbows and briefcases digging into them on all sides. Spike just managed to move his head in time to prevent an umbrella being pushed into his mouth.

When the train stopped at Piccadilly Circus, the crowd carried Wally and the others forward towards an escalator which stretched upwards like an automatic ladder to heaven.

"Stay behind me," Wally said as he reached the first step of the escalator. Spike and the others crowded on behind him.

"Judging by the length of this escalator, we must be miles under the ground," said Doreen.

"Hundreds of yards rather than miles," Wally laughed.

Brunhilde heard none of this. She was too busy reading the framed advertisements that lined the walls. Every so often she would recognise a performer's name, or the name of a place, or the name of a show and give a little squeal and say, "Oh my, we've just got to see him!" or "Oh my, we've just got to go there!" or "Oh my, we simply must go and see that!"

By the time they reached the ticket barrier, it was clear that Brunhilde would need four years instead of four days to do all the things she wanted to do. But then, she had probably brought enough clothes to last her that long.

The choice of exits to street level was multiple. Wally headed for the one closest at hand, which brought them out almost in the middle of Piccadilly Circus.

Spike and Doreen and the Professor recognised it at once from the pictures and films they had seen of it but they had been totally unprepared for the number of people and the roar of the traffic and the feeling of energy and speed.

"Where's the big top?" Brunhilde asked. "You know, for the circus."

Wally laughed. "It's not that kind of circus. Here the word means a circle, a roundabout."

"Well, for heaven's sake, how silly..." Brunhilde began to say. Then her words trailed away as she looked at the building next to them. There were almost life-size statues of Elvis Presley and Michael Jackson and other pop-stars on one of the balconies. "It's a museum of pop-stars and rock!" she squealed. "Oh we've just got to go there!"

"I think you should wait until you are famous," Wally said.

"You mean until there's a statue of me there too?" Brunhilde's eyes glazed over at the idea. "Yes, you're right, Wally. I shouldn't waste my time being just a fan. I should get to work on my songs about London. Now, where are all those tour buses?"

Wally spoke to a passing policeman, "Excuse me, please, but can you tell me where the tour buses leave from?"

"You'll find them just down there, sir, on the left-hand side of the street."

"Thanks very much."

Spike nudged the Professor. "He sounded like an actor on the TV."

"I know," said the Professor, "and this place is like being in a meeting-place of the United Nations."

The others saw what the Professor meant, now that they had got over the first shock of the crowded pavements and the noise. The people who passed by were of every colour, dressed in a huge variety of clothes and speaking more foreign languages than even Brunhilde could try to name.

The place where the tour buses left from was thronged with a similar mixture of people, trying to decide which bus to take. Wally and the others clambered on board the one that offered a recorded commentary in English. It was open-topped and the five of them managed to squeeze into the front seats.

Soon they were part of the great swirl of traffic, weaving in and out past the famous buildings they had seen from the aeroplane.

They went through Trafalgar Square with the National Gallery and Nelson's Column, at whose base dozens of people fed the pigeons, while others soaked their feet in the basins of the fountains.

The bus then went along the Strand and Fleet

Street to St Paul's Cathedral. The commentary told them about the Great Plague and the Fire of London and the Monument that still stood in a side-street to remind people of how the city had been almost totally destroyed.

"Got to climb that," Brunhilde said.

They drove past the Tower of London and across Tower Bridge, where there were now ships and lifts that took visitors to the tops of the towers that flanked each end. "Got to visit that," Brunhilde said.

They drove down a side-street past a queue of people outside a building, with a sign for "The London Dungeon."

"Definitely got to visit *that*," said Brunhilde. "There were posters for that all the way up the escalator."

The bus reached the river and drove along it past Cleopatra's Needle, which, as the commentator pointed out, is not a needle but a huge obelisk brought by sea to London. Across the river were the National Theatre and the Museum of the Moving Image.

Then they were at the Houses of Parliament. Big Ben obligingly sounded the half-hour as they passed.

"Oh my, I'm getting so many good ideas," Brunhilde thrilled.

"So am I," said the Professor.

"You are? What about?"

"I don't know for sure yet. I just wish I'd brought my camera."

"How stupid of us!" Wally said. "I forgot mine too."

"We can borrow one from Jenny," Brunhilde said. "It'll be easier anyway to take pictures when we are on foot."

"On foot? All this distance? That'll take days and days," Spike said.

"Of course, it won't."

Westminster Abbey was next. Then Admiralty Arch and along the Mall towards Buckingham Palace. There was no flag flying over it. According to the commentary, this meant that the Queen was not home.

"Oh, what a shame," Wally said. "We might have called in for a cup of tea!"

The bus drove on through Chelsea, past Harrods and Hyde Park Corner and back to the starting point.

Doreen, Spike and Wally felt as though they had been on a roller-coaster. The Professor was more quiet in his reaction. Brunhilde was very excited, jumping from one foot to another. "Wow! Wow! Wow! That was terrific! But we mustn't waste any time! First the London

Dungeon! We'll spend some of our money on a taxi!"

She spun around looking for a cab. Then she paused, posed and smiled. "There's someone wanting to take my picture! It could be someone who was at the Curragh races!"

"It's the man from the hotel!" the Professor said. "He must have been on the bus! That means he must have followed us from the house in Regent's Park! He knows where we are staying!"

The idea so frightened the Professor that he spoke his thoughts out loud, not caring who heard them.

Spike too decided that the matter was now too serious not to include Brunhilde in the affair. "This man keeps turning up wherever we go. We don't know who he is."

"Well, let's ask him," Brunhilde said. "I can still see him."

Before they could stop her, Brunhilde pushed her way through the crowd. The others ran after her. Wally called out, "Brunhilde, will you come back out of that!"

A group of tall black Africans, dressed in brightly-coloured robes, momentarily obscured Wally's view of the street. "Sorry. So sorry," the Africans smiled. "We need to get to the tour bus!"

"Yes, of course," Wally managed to say as they pushed past each other. Spike, the Professor and Doreen skirted them and made as if to go after Brunhilde. "Don't all go rushing off." Wally grabbed out at them. "Stay together or we'll never find each other again."

A new movement of people put Spike out of Wally's reach. Suddenly Spike heard Brunhilde shouting, "Where are you? Hey, you guys, where are you?"

"Over here," Spike called back. "We can't see you."

"I'm at the record shop on the corner!"

There was a brief break in the flow of people as traffic-lights changed. Spike caught sight of Brunhilde. "Stay there." He turned and looked for the others as he spoke. Wally was towering over the crowd. "She's over here!"

"Stay with her!" Wally shouted. "Don't move, either of you!"

But by the time Spike reached Brunhilde, the lights had once more changed. Traffic rushed forward separating Spike and Brunhilde from the others. "Are you crazy to run off like that after a complete stranger?" Spike demanded.

"He can't be that much of a stranger if you keep seeing him all the time! I don't think he was on the bus tour. I think he saw us get on it and just waited for us to come back. He's hiding in a doorway just along there, waiting to make sure that the coast is clear."

As if to prove that Brunhilde was telling the truth, the man chose that moment to stick his head out. Brunhilde pulled Spike flat against the wall. "I don't think he saw us," Brunhilde said. "No, he didn't. He's on the move again!"

The man was hurrying away from the two young people.

Brunhilde set off after him.

"You've got to wait for Wally and the others," Spike said. Then, as Brunhilde ignored him, he reached out and grabbed her arm. "You've got to wait! We promised our parents to stay out of trouble!"

"But the man is getting away!"

Wally and the others had caught up with them by now. For an instant, it felt as though there was going to be a terrific quarrel with everyone shouting at everyone else. Then Wally said, "We are letting our feelings run away with us. We need a cool drink, somewhere to sit, and a nice quiet talk!"

All of those needs were easily and quickly satisfied. There was a fast-food establishment close to where they stood. They trooped inside and at once felt the need not only for a cool drink but for a hot hamburger.

"Call it an early lunch," said Wally, as they lined up and gave their order.

8
What's Going On?

hey selected a table by the window so that they could keep watch on the street in case the man came back. Wally said that no-one should talk for three minutes just to give them all a chance to calm down

When the three minutes were up, Spike and the Professor were both regretting having said so much in front of Brunhilde.

They tried as best they could to make her believe that nothing of any importance was happening but the girl from Santa Fe was not that easily put off the scent.

"Oh come on," she said. "I've had the feeling for days and days that something was being kept from me."

She shoved the last of her hamburger into her mouth but postponed chewing it until Spike spoke.

"We think that Alice Hopper isn't sure where three of The Tree-Tops are—Scarce, Speedy and the Mole."

"But that means she is sure of where only one of them is," said Brunhilde, "the one who plays the drums, Sticks."

"She may not know where he is either," said Doreen. "After all, it would be very odd to lose three and not four."

"I don't see the logic of that," said the Professor. "At the races on Saturday, she managed simply to lose Speedy and the Mole." Then he paused and thought. "Or did she, in fact, lose any of them?"

"What do you mean by that?" asked Spike.

"She only thought she lost them. In fact, they came down to the Curragh with their friends in a different helicopter. Do you not remember the way she spoke to us when she thought we were the Mole and Speedy? It was as though they were forever running off and not doing what they were told. That was why she was so cross last Saturday."

"And do you think that's what's happened again?" asked Doreen. "Do you think that all The Tree-Tops, including Sticks, have run off? That they are hiding somewhere to get away from

Alice?"

"But the big concert is tomorrow evening," said Brunhilde. "If they were going to sneak off anywhere, surely it would be to London! No matter how much they dislike Alice—and I must admit I find her a bit bossy myself—The Tree-Tops would never disappoint their fans by simply not turning up."

"They could still turn up for the concert," Wally said. "It's not as though it's the first concert of their tour. They'll be singing the same songs. They will use the same people to control the lights and the sound system. They could, if they wanted to, arrive just minutes before the concert is due to start and walk on the stage. Maybe they just decided that they wanted a few days to themselves."

"But who is the man that keeps following us around?" Doreen asked.

"He could be a private detective hired by Alice to try and find Scarce and the others."

"Why would a detective looking for The Tree-Tops want to take our photographs?"

"Oh, they always take photographs," said Brunhilde.

"Do you mean you've been followed by private detectives before this?" Even Wally was staring open-mouthed at Brunhilde now.

"Well, no, not exactly," Brunhilde was sad to have to confess that her knowledge of private detectives came from films. "But they do it just to prove that they have been following whoever it is they were told to follow."

An idea came to Doreen. "Maybe he thinks Spike and the Professor swopped places with Speedy and the Mole! Maybe he thinks you two are The Tree-Tops disguised as Spike and the Professor!"

"Then, which of us does he think Scarce is disguised as?" asked Brunhilde.

"Maybe Alice is on the trail of Scarce. Maybe he's still in Dublin and she was rushing off to follow up some kind of clue this morning while the detective looks for Speedy and the Mole in London!"

"And maybe we should get on with the sightseeing," said Wally. "We can talk all this out with Alice when she arrives from Dublin this afternoon."

"*If* she arrives from Dublin this afternoon," corrected Brunhilde, as they walked back out into the dazzling sunshine. "My word, how warm it is, almost as hot as New Mexico."

"Just let's all stay together now," Wally reminded them.

"And keep a careful look-out for the man

with the camera," added Brunhilde.

Then she put her fingers in her mouth and made a piercing whistling sound that made a passing taxi skid to a stop. "The London Dungeon," she said to the driver. "And step on it!"

Brunhilde was obviously not going to pass up the opportunity to imitate a character from a thriller and kept looking out through the back window of the taxi as it sped along. "So far so good," she would occasionally mutter. Or, "I think we finally lost the fuzz," or, "Nobody's gonna make me talk."

The taxi driver was quite relieved to get them out of his cab and barely thanked them for the tip that Wally gave him.

The London Dungeon turned out to be even creepier than the posters would have led one to expect. There were all kinds of scenes of torture and murder and plague with the most realistic models that any of the young people had seen. Even the grown-ups looking around seemed impressed by the various scenes.

Brunhilde made everyone even more nervous by constantly jumping away from shadowy corners as though she had seen something terrible hidden there.

But it was when they were on their way

back out into the street that she gave the others the worst fright of all by screaming, "There he is! There he is!"

Wally said angrily, "There is no-one that we know there."

"There is! There is!" insisted Brunhilde. "Only he went back in as soon as he realised that I'd seen him. Now is our chance to tackle him. Spike, you and the Professor stand guard here. Doreen and Wally and I will spread out and check the inside."

"No, you won't," said Wally. "How could the man even know we were coming here?"

"He told another taxi to follow us!" Brunhilde said.

"More likely he heard Brunhilde giving directions in that loud voice to the driver of our taxi," Spike said. "He must have been hiding near where we were."

"Even if we did find him in there, which is very unlikely if he doesn't want to be found, what are we going to do then?" asked Wally. "He has as much right to be here as we have. He doesn't have to answer our questions. We just have to stick to our agreement not to do anything until we speak to Alice. Now, we can walk across the bridge to the Tower of London from here. You really ought to see that."

There was a long queue waiting to go inside the Tower. The sun beat relentlessly down on them. Slowly they moved forward.

Their guide was a fine figure of a man dressed in the uniform of the Beefeaters, the guardians of the Tower of London. The story he told of how the Tower had been founded and of the people who had been imprisoned there was fascinating, yet to Wally and his companions, it was as though they were hearing it from a distance. The heat of the day probably had something to do with this. Or the fact that they had been up so early in the day and done so much rushing around. Or it could have had to do with the realisation that they were just filling in time until it was time to go back to Jenny's house and wait for Alice Hopper.

9
Alice Arrives

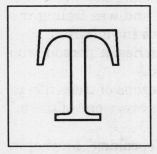he only moving air in the entire city seemed to be at the mouth of the tunnels in the underground stations. People who were used to London stood at the end of the platforms and briefly enjoyed its soothing touch before they pushed their way on to the train.

Doreen said, "Now I know what it's like to be in a rugby scrum."

When at last they emerged, or rather *fell* onto the platform of Regent's Park station, they all felt exhausted and would have sat down if Brunhilde, still playing at being followed, hadn't said, "OK, you guys, keep moving. We don' wanna take no chances so close to home."

The fact that there was no-one else on the platform or in the lift to street level didn't stop Brunhilde from behaving like a fugitive from justice.

Faced with the sun-baked spaces of the park itself, she paused and said, "Every tree could shelter a watcher."

"What's a what-cher?" asked the Professor, who was very fair-skinned and was feeling the effects of the heat more than the others.

"Not a what-cher, a watcher, a person who watches," Brunhilde replied.

"There are dozens and dozens of trees. There couldn't be a watcher under every one of them," said Spike.

"I meant 'in a manner of speaking'. Maybe we should split up and cause confusion."

"We have more than enough confusion to go on with," Wally said, "without us all going off in different directions. And as we have already agreed, we are going to stick together until we talk to Alice."

"That's boring," Brunhilde said.

"You just want to go off and try to claim all the credit for yourself," said Spike.

"No I don't."

"OK, OK," Wally said. "Let's save our energy for the walk back to the house. It should be over there, in that direction."

"No, it's not," said Brunhilde. "It's over *there*. I remember that kind of tea-room building.

That was on our left when we set out so it has to be on our right on the way back."

"You're both wrong," said Doreen. "Jenny's and Daly's houses are over *there*."

"Maybe we should go by the road," the Professor said, who really was longing to get indoors as quickly as possible. "We passed the zoo this morning in the car. There's a sign here that points to the zoo."

"Hey, that's right," Brunhilde said admiringly. "And the road is probably the safest anyway."

"I wish you wouldn't keep going on as though we were in some terrible danger," Spike said.

"London is a city of danger," Brunhilde said. "And that's what one of my new songs is going to be called. 'London, where danger lurks'."

Before anyone could stop her, she began to sing to exactly the same tune as all her other songs,

> London is a city of danger
> And nothing will ever change her
> Until we find poor Scarce
> The shadows melt and tremble
> And seem to soon resemble
> The man we all must fear
> As he goes CLICK CLICK
> With his camera.

"I thought," said Wally, "that the intention was not to attract attention."

"I don't recall anyone saying that," said Brunhilde. "The more people look at us, the safer we are from our enemies."

Before Wally could argue the sense behind that statement, the Professor said in a dazed voice, "I'm sorry. Maybe it's the sun, but I think I've just seen a sheep on top of a mountain."

The others stared sorrowfully at the Professor. "Maybe we should sit down and cover his head with our hands," said Doreen, looking around for a suitable place. Then she gave a slight scream. "A giraffe! I've just seen a giraffe!"

Spike, thoroughly alarmed now, said, "Can sun-stroke be catching? Could someone have put something in our food?"

That suggestion brought Wally to his senses. He looked around. "It's all part of the zoo," he said. "There's an artificial mountain in there behind the railings with a long-horned sheep on top of it. If you look over here, you can see the head of the giraffe, sticking up over the fence. We are all letting our imagination run-away with us. Now then, no more nonsense and no more singing."

"Well, of course, if you don't want to be able to tell your friends that you were among the very first to hear my new song," Brunhilde said crossly.

"I'd much sooner be able to tell them that we all got back safely to Jenny South's house. So let's do that. We can't be very far from it now."

Wally was right. The two houses were less than five minutes' walk away. The gates swung open as soon as they had identified themselves on the intercom and were surveyed by the security cameras.

Peter Arnew opened the front door. "Well, you certainly look as though you've had a busy day. Mr. Daly and the two ladies got back just a few minutes ago. We are all going to have tea in the drawing-room."

Stepping inside Jenny South's house was like going from one world into another. It was so quiet and dark and cool.

"Air-conditioning," Brunhilde said. "I didn't think they had air-conditioning in England."

"It's becoming more common as the summers seem to get hotter and longer."

"Did you get The Tree-Tops' telephone number for me?"

"I think Amanda has it. She's inside with the others."

But, before Brunhilde could repeat her question to Amanda, the grown ups' attention focused on the Professor. "You've got far too much sun," Amanda said. "You should have worn a hat."

"I'm grand now that I'm in the cool," the Professor said.

"No, no, you're not. You need some kind of cream for your face. Doesn't he, Mrs O'Brien?"

"He certainly does."

"But I go out in the sun all the time at home in Dublin." Then he paused and remembered how his mother would try and make him put on suntan lotion before he left the house. Usually he managed not to hear her but he couldn't avoid hearing Amanda.

She said, "I'm sure Miss South has something upstairs that would do. Peter, you don't think she would mind if I looked, do you?"

"No, of course not. Let me come and show you which room is hers."

The secretaries hurried out of the room as two maids wheeled in the tea trolley. Martin Daly rubbed his hands in delight. "Boys, oh boys," he said. "This is just the ticket."

Even Mrs Hurt and Granny O'Brien were impressed by the wonderful array of sandwiches and pastries and the beautiful teaset. Brunhilde took a sandwich. Mrs Hurt said, "I think we should wait for Amanda and Peter to come back."

Brunhilde said, "Sorry. It's just that whenever I need to think I find that food helps. So when I saw the food here, I took some without thinking."

"Well now that perhaps the food has started you thinking, you'll not touch anything else until everyone is here."

"What kind of day did you have?" Wally asked, anxious to keep the peace.

"Oh wonderful," Granny O'Brien said. "A glimpse of the past."

For a moment, it looked as though she and Mrs. Hurt were going to have what they called "a bit of a weep", but somehow they shrugged it away. "You won't believe it but some of the people we knew over fifty years ago were still living in the same place. And not only that, but they remembered us!"

"And who could forget two such charming ladies?" asked Martin.

"Oh no, Martin, none of your flattery," Granny O'Brien said but it was easy to see that she and Mrs Hurt were delighted. "Sure weren't you remembered in those pubs you brought us to?"

"Ah yes, but for rather different reasons," Martin said. "The people there remembered me as a fool who gambled all his money away. And it wasn't fifty years since they'd seen me."

"All the same, they were glad to see you again and to hear about your great fortune in meeting your long-lost cousin, Daly Carson," Mrs Hurt said.

"Did anyone try to take your photograph?" Brunhilde asked, reaching for another sandwich and then remembering, just in time, that she was supposed to wait.

"Not that I recall," said Granny O'Brien, "except that there was one man with a camera. I noticed him in one of the pubs. He kept looking at us. I thought he recognised Martin but he made no attempt to speak to him."

"Was the man kind of fat with hair turning grey?"

"No, more blonde and going bald."

"I recall him too," Martin said. "In fact, I was on the point of going up to ask him who he thought he was looking at when he finished his drink and left."

"It wasn't the same man then," Brunhilde said.

"The same man as who?" asked Granny O'Brien.

"Oh, just a man we saw in the West End," Wally said quickly, hoping the matter would be forgotten. But Brunhilde was not to be stopped.

"And in the hotel in Dublin and at the

airports in Dublin and in London…and at the London Dungeon." She recited the places like a litany.

Spike and Doreen and the Professor were furious with her. How could she be so stupid! Not only could she be the cause of them not being allowed out again but she could ruin the old people's weekend by making them worry!

"I'll bet the man you saw in the pub is working with the fellow we keep seeing. It all has to do with the same mystery!" Brunhilde exclaimed.

"What mystery?" Amanda and Peter were standing at the door of the drawing room.

"Brunhilde thinks we are all being followed," Mrs O'Brien said.

"Oh, and what makes her think that?" Peter asked.

"Because we keep seeing the same man, that's why," said Brunhilde. "And there was a second man watching Martin and Mrs Hurt and Granny O'Brien."

Amanda handed the Professor a tube of cream. "Rub it evenly on your face. On your arms as well. Maybe you'd be better to do it in one of the bathrooms."

"He can do it in ours," Brunhilde said. "Oh and could I have The Tree-Tops' telephone number?"

Amanda took a piece of paper from her pocket. "The number is 091-222 4900. But it's the telephone number for Sticks, the drummer. The other members don't live in London."

A servant came into the room. "Excuse me, please. Miss Hopper has just arrived by taxi."

"I hope she remembered my luggage." Martin hurried forward to meet Alice, who looked tired and even more worried than usual.

"Yes, yes," she said before Martin could ask the question. "Your luggage is in the hall."

"Come and sit down," Mrs Hurt said to Alice. "You look as though you could do with a nice cup of tea. In fact we all could. I'll pour. Amanda will pass and no-one will speak for three minutes."

The young people smiled when they heard Mrs Hurt give the same instruction as Wally had earlier on. He had obviously learned from his grandmother that this was the easiest way to calm people down.

The passing of the minutes was marked by the loud ticking of a clock, of which until then the young people had been unaware. The sound made the drawing-room somehow quieter and even more cool. When the period of silence finished, everyone felt much better. Mrs Hurt began to pour tea. Amanda passed the cups. Peter passed the food. Granny O'Brien said. "Now then, Alice, what exactly is going on? Brunhilde has been dropping all kinds of hints that we are involved in some great mystery."

Alice drained her tea-cup, held it out for a refill, sighed, and told the following story.

When The Tree-Tops started their tour of Ireland and Great Britain, Alice had been hired to look after the publicity for the group and also to look after the group itself. At first everything had gone very well. The concerts had been well attended. There had been very little trouble at any of them. But then the weather had started to get hotter and hotter. Audiences had got noisier and noisier. Travelling from one place to another had taken longer and longer as more and more people took to the roads to visit the seaside or even just to find a nice, quiet field to sit in.

Matters became even worse when The Tree-Tops' record got to the number one position in the Top Twenty. Then people who, before this, might not have wanted to hear the group in a concert, now wanted to buy tickets.

Extra concerts were arranged, which was, as Alice now agreed, a great mistake; everyone ended up very tired and very cross. By the time Alice and The Tree-Tops got to Ireland, Speedy and the Mole were saying that they could not put up with much more of it.

Speedy had said, "It's like living in a glass cage. I want some time to myself."

The Mole had agreed.

On the morning of the big race meeting on the Curragh, Speedy and the Mole left the hotel early. Alice couldn't find them anywhere. They had not turned up at a special lunch. They were supposed to be giving an interview to Harry Speakes, a very important journalist, who was furious when only two of the group had shown up.

Alice was so worried she might lose her job that she had mistaken Spike and the Professor for the Mole and Speedy at the Curragh.

"And that's when things really started to go wrong," Alice said.

"But how can that be?" asked the Professor. "I know that there was a lot of confusion but surely everything worked out all right? Everyone seemed perfectly happy and contented at Wally's disco."

"It was the next morning that I was thinking of," said Alice. "That was when the group really started to get difficult. It is as though the taste of freedom that they got at Wally's disco made them more unhappy. And this time it wasn't just Speedy and the Mole. It was Scarce as well. I had persuaded Harry Speakes to make another appointment to talk to the boys. His articles are published in newspapers all over the world. Thousands of people read him in America, where The Tree-Tops are going very soon.

"Harry agreed to stay over in Dublin and talk to them on Monday afternoon. Three o'clock came. The only one of the group to turn up was Sticks. At first we thought that the others would come along but they didn't, so I went up to their suite to look for them. They weren't there. Sticks said he hadn't seen them since breakfast-time. Harry was furious. He said he'd write an article that would tell everyone how spoiled and nasty Scarce and Speedy and the Mole were."

"Gee!" said Brunhilde. "You'd think he'd understand that the boys just didn't feel like being interviewed."

"And at least Sticks was there," said Doreen.

"Sticks is very shy. He never has anything to say. Harry got the idea that, because Sticks wasn't a good talker, he was hiding something. He began to suspect that something had happened to Scarce and the others."

"Do you mean that they might have been kidnapped?" asked Spike.

"Yes. I tried tc tell him that it wasn't true..."

"But, are you sure it wasn't...I mean isn't

true?" asked Brunhilde.

"Of course I'm sure. We'd have heard from the kidnappers by now."

"Maybe they got in touch with Scarce's parents and warned them against saying anything," Doreen suggested. "Have you been in touch with them?"

The two secretaries and Alice exchanged a long look. Then Alice said, "I don't see that it matters if we tell you now. It's going to be made public fairly soon anyway. Jenny South is Scarce's mother. Before Jenny became famous, she was married to a young man from her home town in the North of England. A year after Scarce was born, there was a terrible road accident. Scarce's father was killed. It was after that that Jenny decided to work really hard at becoming a well-known actress. She needed the money. At the same time, she wanted Scarce to have as normal a childhood as possible. While she was off working in London and in Hollywood, he was looked after by his grandparents. Jenny spent as much time as she could with him and never mentioned him to the press. Later on, when Scarce began to play the guitar and started The Tree-Tops, he never mentioned that Jenny was his mother. He wanted to be a success on his own and not because he was Jenny South's son. That was why he came to Ireland. It wasn't just to go to the races. It was to talk to Jenny about a plan he had to make a record with her. She's got a lovely singing voice."

"Jenny South and The Tree-Tops on the same record!" said Brunhilde. "Wow! And I think that I might have the very song for them. It's called 'Parents are a Dog's Best Friend.' It goes like this..."

But before Brunhilde could sing the opening words of her song, the others all told her to be quiet and let Alice go on with her story.

"There isn't very much more," Alice said. "Sticks doesn't know where the other three fellows are. None of the hotel staff knew for sure when they'd last seen them. The hotel was so crowded that that was understandable. I checked everywhere that I could think of, telephoned anyone that they might know in Ireland. I got no information as to where they might be. Scarce and Speedy and the Mole have just vanished. I waited for almost forty-eight hours before I got in touch with Jenny. The big concert is tomorrow evening."

"But surely they will turn up," said Granny O'Brien. "They would never be foolish enough to throw away all that they've worked for."

"I've seen it happen before," Alice said. "There was a singer called Johnson Parrott, who was a great success a few years ago. He couldn't stand the problems of being a pop-star. He walked out of a concert that he was giving. Later on, when he wanted to start singing again, no-one would give him work. The very same thing could happen to The Tree-Tops, especially if it gets around that Jenny is Scarce's mother. They will blame her as much as Scarce. People like Harry Speakes will say that Scarce is a spoiled brat."

"And, really, all he and the others are are three young men who found that being famous is not all that it's cracked up to be," said Martin.

"Does that mean you're changing your mind about becoming an actor?" asked Mrs Hurt.

"No, no. I think, at my age, I can cope with fame and fortune," Martin replied.

"If they would only do tomorrow night's concert, they could decide the future without harming anyone. I'm just afraid that they are going to cut off their noses to spite their faces," Alice moaned.

Brunhilde said, "Talking of noses and faces, we'd better put that cream on the Professor."

"Oh yes," said Amanda. "We were forgetting about that."

"Don't worry. Leave it to us. We'll do it

upstairs."

"Oh by the way," Peter said. "Miss South and Mr. Daly have to work late at the studio. They suggested we all go out to dinner at our local Greek restaurant."

"A Greek restaurant sounds great," said Brunhilde. "I bet we'll be able to dance." She gave a brief display of what she imagined Greek dancing might be like.

10
Brunhilde Runs Off

he first thing Brunhilde did in the bedroom was to switch on the TV. Then she opened the window to let in the sound of traffic. "In case of spies in the house," she said.

"Spies in the house!" Doreen was shocked.

"Yes, spies! Someone has been giving out information about our movements to Harry Speakes."

"Do you mean that the man we keep seeing is Harry Speakes?" The Professor's feeling of dizziness was returning. He sat on the edge of a bed.

"Of course! Who else could it be? I more or less guessed he was a journalist from the first time I saw him. I even said so to you."

"You say lots of things that aren't necessarily true," said Spike.

"No, but I hit the jackpot this time," Brunhilde

laughed.

Doreen said, "You almost sound pleased that Scarce and the others are going to ruin their careers."

"No, I'm just pleased that I am going to have the chance to *save* their careers."

"Save them?" Alarm bells began to ring in Spike's mind. Every fibre of his being told him that major trouble was looming. "We promised not to get into trouble."

"Since when is helping someone called getting into trouble?" demanded Brunhilde. "And anyway, think of how grateful they will be."

"By which you mean they will sit down and listen to your songs," snapped Spike.

"And what's wrong with that? One of the chief reasons I came to London was so that Scarce would hear my music."

"You still can't go around taking advantage of people," Doreen said.

"I'm not doing that," Brunhilde replied. "But before we do anything else, I think we should put some of that cream on the Professor's face. He looks like a tomato that's about to burst."

The Professor felt that way too. His head throbbed and the idea of coping with one of Brunhilde's madcap schemes made him want to just lie down and sleep.

"Sit up straight," Doreen said, and wrapped a towel around his neck. Then she gently began to smooth cream over his face. The cream vanished like water being soaked up by a sponge.

"Put some more on him," said Brunhilde. "Lots and lots and lots."

Doreen gave the Professor's face a second, then a third coating, then a fourth, by which time the tube was empty and the Professor felt much, much better. "That's great," he said.

"Good. Now all of you sit there while I make a telephone call." Brunhilde unfolded the piece of paper with Sticks's telephone number on it and dialled it on the telephone on the bedside table.

There was an immediate answer.

"Hi there, Sticks. You must have been sitting next to the phone, waiting for it to ring."

"Who is this?" Sticks asked.

"Why it's Brunhilde Brisk, of course."

"Oh yeh, the American girl."

"That's right. My friends and I were wondering if we could come and see you."

"What do you want to see me about?"

"Why, about Scarce and the Mole and Speedy, of course."

"You know where they are?"

"No, not exactly, but I have a terrific plan only I can't talk about it on the phone."

"Where are you speaking from?"

"Jenny South's house in Regent's Park."

"I'm not too far away from there. Have you a pencil and paper?"

There was a note pad and a pencil next to the phone. Brunhilde scribbled down the directions that Sticks gave her. "See you in a few minutes," she said and hung up. "We can walk to his place from here."

The Professor said, "I don't think I want to go back out into all that heat just yet."

"That's all right. Spike and Doreen and myself can manage without you."

"Manage to do what?" asked Spike. "I'm not moving from here until you tell me."

"In that event, you'd better stay. Doreen, you're coming, aren't you?"

"Yes, if Granny O'Brien and Wally think it's OK."

"Oh fiddle-de-dee," Brunhilde said. "They would never understand my plan. See you all later."

Before the others could move, Brunhilde was gone from the room. Doreen ran after her. "Brunhilde, you mustn't go off on your own."

Doreen reached the landing just in time to see Brunhilde go through the door that led to the back stairs. "Please, Brunhilde!" Doreen called out. "You must come back."

Brunhilde gave no sign that she had heard Doreen. Instead, she opened the door at the foot of the stairs and found herself in the kitchen. The two maids who had wheeled in the tea trolley looked up, startled, from their own tea. "Can we get you something?" one of them asked.

"I need to go on a very important errand. It's a surprise," Brunhilde said. "Is there another way out of the house?"

"There's the side-entrance where deliveries are made."

"That sounds ideal. Can you open it for me?"

"Yes, if you want me to." One of the maids took a key off a hook and led Brunhilde out into the back garden. She turned the key in the side-entrance and keyed in the security code. The door clicked open. Doreen, followed by the second maid, came rushing out of the house. She once more called, "Please, Brunhilde! You must come back."

But Brunhilde once more ignored Doreen and ran off down the side of the house. Doreen followed her, still shouting, "Please, Brunhilde!"

The two maids stared at each other in bewilderment. "Should we go and tell Mr Arnew?" the one with the key asked.

But Peter Arnew and the grown-ups had no

need to be told, for Spike had just come rushing into the drawing-room. "Where is she? Where's Brunhilde? And Doreen?"

"Don't tell me they've vanished as well!" Thoroughly alarmed, Granny O'Brien got to her feet.

"You mean you didn't see them?" Spike made for the hall door as the two maids ran in from the kitchen. "Have you seen my sister and Brunhilde?"

"They ran off! The tall one made me open the side entrance."

"Is it still open?" Spike asked.

"Yes," the maid said, and jumped back as Spike galloped towards the kitchen, leaving behind him a chorus of cautions and protests.

Upstairs, on the landing, the Professor, still woozy from the sun, tried to decide what to do for the best. He doubted that he could run fast enough to catch up with Spike and the girls even if he knew where they were going. The grown-ups seemed to be in a similar state to judge from the babble of voices. Then there was the sound of definite movement. The front door opened and closed. The car, parked outside, stirred into life. As it drove off, the Professor heard other footsteps make for the kitchen. The grown-ups must have split into two groups, one to go by car, the other on foot. But, go where?

How would they know where to go? Even he didn't know where Brunhilde had gone to...

He turned and there, on the carpet, was the page from the pad with Sticks's address on it: Number Seventeen, Crofton Street. Brunhilde had dropped it in her eagerness to get away. The question was, would she remember the address without the sheet?

If she didn't, whatever plan she had could fail because she did not have Sticks's address. She and Doreen and Spike were running through the streets of London followed by a car of grown-ups, plus several more on foot. And yet it was possible that he, and he alone, knew where everyone ought to be going.

He went down the main staircase as quickly as possible. The two maids were standing in the hall, confused and worried, unable to decide what they should do next.

"Where is Crofton Street?" the Professor asked.

"It's about ten minutes' walk away from here," the taller of the maids said.

"Can you draw me a map on the back of this?" The Professor handed her the sheet from the pad.

"Oh yes, I think so. I have a pencil in the kitchen—only, please, what is happening? My sister here and I, we are so worried."

"I'm not sure exactly what's wrong," the

Professor replied. "But none of it is your fault."

"Oh yes, it is," the maid said, as she took a pencil out of a drawer and began to sketch a map on the back of Sticks's address. "Maria and I, we open the side-entrance for the big one."

"Brunhilde? The tall American?"

"Yes. And the other girl, she run off that way as well..."

"And also the boy with the sticking-up hair," said Maria. "Oh, Dolores, what have we done!"

A telephone in the kitchen gave a loud ring, making the three of them jump. With trembling hand, Maria answered it. She became even more upset. "It is security. They say that we forgot to close the side entrance. There is a light on on their panel."

"If I go out that way, would it be quicker?" the Professor asked.

"Yes," said Maria. She pointed to the finished map. "Turn right and you will end up here."

"Good," said the Professor.

Maria and Dolores followed him across the garden. As they reached the side entrance, Harry Speakes came into view. He had a camera in his hand. "Hold it right there," he said.

"You are trespassing," Maria declared. "Go away!"

"Not until I ask a few questions."

"Such as what, Mr. Speakes?" the Professor said.

Harry was taken by surprise to hear his name used. "How did you know who I..."

But, before he could finish, the Professor had pushed past him and the maids bolted the door. It took Harry a few seconds to regain his balance and to go after the boy, who was running in a very slow, lopsided manner.

Harry caught up with him quite easily and, in spite of being fat, managed to puff out a few words as he jogged alongside him. "There's no good trying to get away. I know there's something going on here, something really big."

"Leave us alone," the Professor said.

"After wasting nearly a whole week following you lot around?"

"How do you know it was us you were following?"

"How do I know what? I happen to be one of the best reporters when it comes to showbusiness. Or maybe you are going to pretend that you are not aware of that?"

"I'm only aware that you are trying to make trouble for a lot of very nice people," the Professor said.

"Oh, and I suppose they haven't been making trouble for me? I suppose they haven't been not turning up for interviews? I suppose that they haven't been making me feel so foolish that only a really, big, exclusive story will make things better for me? Oh and when I say exclusive, I mean exclusive, not like the story about The Tree-Tops that got into every newspaper last week-end!"

The rapid manner in which Harry spoke was, to the Professor, like being thumped with a rolled-up newspaper. The sun blazed down on him as he left the shade of the houses and the trees and reached the main road. It was like being back in Piccadilly Circus. It was all too much. He stumbled and fell. Harry tripped over him, losing his grip on his camera.

The camera slid across the pavement and out on to the road, where a lorry ran over it.

11
Trouble in Traffic

everal minutes before Harry's camera was squashed Wally, Amanda and Peter arrived on the main road. They rushed out the side entrance of Jenny's house in pursuit of the young people, while Alice and the older people ordered Ned to drive around the area in search of what Alice now thought of as the runaways.

The car and its occupants were now stuck in traffic, unable to even turn around to go back to the house. To make matters worse, the hot weather had affected the car phone. All efforts to contact Maria and Dolores, to see if the runaways had returned, ended in failure. The phone just went dead before Alice finished dialling the number

"And to think it was working all right this

morning," Mrs Hurt said. "I remember seeing Fred use it as we drove along!"

Alice's face hardened. "As you drove along where?"

"As we were on our way to visit the places we used to know," Mrs Hurt replied. "You are not suggesting that Fred was phoning that journalist fellow to tell him where we were going?"

Martin became equally angry. He slid back the glass panel that divided the passenger area from the front seats. "Have you been giving out information to the newspapers about us?" he demanded of Fred.

Fred was amazed by the accusation. "Why, no, Mr Daly! Miss South would never forgive me if I did such a thing."

"Then who were you talking to on the phone this morning?"

"It was the detective that Miss South hired."

"A detective?"

"Yes. As far as I understand it, there's a problem over The Tree-Tops. Miss South was worried so she hired this detective."

"Hold on a second," Granny O'Brien said. "What does the detective look like?"

"I don't know. I never saw him. He got in touch with me on the car phone."

"Are you thinking what I'm thinking?" asked

Granny O' Brien. "That was no detective. That was the bald blonde man who was in the pub. He's working for Harry Speakes and not Jenny South! Fred, surely you could have checked his story."

"Ordinarily I would," Fred said. "But Miss South's been so busy since she got back from Ireland. Not once has she been alone in the car. There's always been someone talking about the TV series or her future plans. And anyway this detective seemed to know so much and what he asked me to do seemed very unimportant. He just wanted me to let him know where you and the children were going to in case any member of The Tree-Tops contacted you. I feel such a fool now!"

"Don't worry. You did what you thought was best. Miss South and Daly Carson will understand," Martin said. "If only this traffic would move, we'd be fine."

"Where exactly is it we are going to?" Granny O'Brien asked.

Much the same question was being asked by Doreen as, with one final burst of speed, she caught up with Brunhilde.

"You know well where I'm going. I'm going to see Sticks," Brunhilde replied.

"That's *who* you are going to see, not *where*,"

Doreen said.

"I have the address written down here. We should turn to the left fairly soon now." Brunhilde fumbled about in the left-hand pocket of her jeans. Then she fumbled in the right-hand pocket, then in the two back pockets, then in the pocket of her tee-shirt. For a second, it looked as though she might take her trainers off and look inside them. "I've lost the address!" she shrieked. "I don't know where it is!"

Spike reached the two girls. "You're both in big trouble with the grown-ups," he panted.

"That is as nothing compared to the problem we have right here," said Brunhilde. "I've lost Sticks's address. Oh, and here come Wally and the secretaries. We'll just have to take a chance that I recognise the name of the road. It was something like Crimpton Road."

"The name of the road wouldn't be Chingford Road, would it? That's the name of the road on the other side."

"Yes, yes, that sounds very like it," Brunhilde said. "And the number is seventeen. I remember that because it's the same number as the O'Neills' house in Dublin."

The three young people dodged through the stalled traffic and down Chingford Road. Number Seventeen was the fifth house on the left.

Its windows were so dirty that it would be impossible to see either in or out of them. The front door, badly in need of painting, had a huge padlock attached to it. "This can't be the right place," Spike said.

"What's that lying against the dustbins?" Doreen asked.

Spike turned around a sign attached to a long pole. The words on the sign were "For Sale. All Enquiries to Flogem and Lets, Estate Agents."

"Not only does Sticks not live here but, by the looks of it, no-one lives here or would want to," said Spike.

A pounding of feet on the pavement made Spike drop the sign. "Oh it's you," he said, as Amanda and Peter and Wally arrived outside the house.

"Well, you certainly picked a terrific time to go house-hunting," Peter said.

"We're not house-hunting," Spike said, treating Peter's attempt at a joke as serious. "Brunhilde lost the address of where Sticks lives."

"Sticks lives on Crofton Road," Peter said. "Over the greengrocer's. I've often given Scarce a lift there."

Brunhilde said "Then that is where we must go!" And off she went, but as she reached the middle of the main road there was a sudden movement of traffic, leaving her stranded.

"Thank heavens for that," Peter said. "It might give her time to calm down."

But, instead of becoming calmer, Brunhilde screamed and began to run after a brown car. "They've got him! They've got him!"

"Got who?" The others, thoroughly alarmed, dodged through the traffic and set off after Brunhilde.

A lorry driver yelled, "What cha tryin' to do then? Get yourselves killed?"

Several motors shouted similar questions as Brunhilde drew level with the brown car.

"Oh be careful! Be careful!" pleaded Amanda, narrowly avoiding being hit by a motor cyclist.

The lights ahead began to change. The brown car braked. Brunhilde pulled the back door open and looked in at the Professor on the back seat. "Don't worry. I'm here," she said.

Suddenly the lights changed back to green without ever getting to red. It was this fault on the lights that was causing the traffic jam. The man in the front passenger seat leaned back and pulled Brunhilde into the car. She fell in a heap on top of the Professor. The car shot forward as Brunhilde recognised the man who had dragged her into the car! It was Harry Speakes!

"You won't get away with this," Brunhilde said in her toughest private detective voice. "I've got friends in high places."

"I don't care if all your friends live on top of a mountain," the driver snarled back. "Stop bouncing around back there!"

"The bald blonde!" Brunhilde recognised the driver from the description she had heard in the drawing-room of the man Martin and the others had seen in the pub.

"I'm not *that* bald," the man said crossly.

"Oh yes, you are! You look like a snooker ball with a ribbon tied around it! And you won't get away with trying to kidnap us!"

"They're not trying to kidnap us," the Professor said, recovering from the shock of being sat on by Brunhilde.

"I pulled you into the car to save you from being run over by that crazy motor cyclist," Harry Speakes said. "He was headed straight for you."

"Look out!" yelled the Professor.

Traffic had ground to a halt at yet another set of faulty traffic lights, whose timing mechanism had been affected, like the car phone, by the heat. The balding blonde slammed on his brakes. As the car swerved to a stop, a motorcyclist cut out in front of it. The bumper of the car touched the back mudguard of the motor bike.

"It's that same crazy guy that almost ran over you," said Harry. "It's a good thing Samuel has his wits about him."

"Who is Samuel?" asked Brunhilde.

"I am," said the driver.

"I love the name Samuel," Brunhilde said. "I once wrote a song about a bear called Samuel. It was one of my less good songs. The words were never quite right. Hey, maybe I should have called it 'Samuel, the bear with no hair'!"

Samuel was furious and would have said so, but he had a new problem to deal with. The motor cyclist had jumped off his machine to examine the rear mudguard. It was impossible to see his face because of the helmet he wore but he was quite big and strong-looking. He approached the car.

Samuel rolled down the window. "Hello there," he said, hopefully. "No damage done, thank heavens."

"That's for me to decide," the motor cyclist replied in a surprisingly high-pitched voice.

The traffic lights changed to green. There was an immediate blaring of horns from the cars behind. "Drive on," Harry said. "I've no time for this nonsense." To the motorcyclist, he said, "Move your machine. There's nothing wrong with it."

"Yeh," said Brunhilde. "Clear the road. We're in a hurry."

There was the sound of voices approaching.

"It's the others," said the Professor. "It's Wally and Doreen and the others."

Harry said to Samuel, "Drive around the motor bike!"

"Oh, no, you don't," said the owner and flung himself across the bonnet of Samuel's car. "Help!" he called to a passing pedal-cyclist. "These people are trying to leave the scene of an accident."

The pedal-cyclist dismounted. Drivers got out of their cars, further slowing down Wally and the others.

"They think they can bang into me and then just drive off," the motorcyclist said.

"You were driving like a lunatic!" Harry got out of the car. "You almost ran this little girl down!"

"I'm no little girl," Brunhilde said. "I am about to become the number one songwriter in the world!"

"You are?" said Harry. "I want to talk to you. Come on! Samuel can deal with this villain."

"Villain! Who's a villain?" demanded the motorbike rider, but Harry was already halfway to the pavement with Brunhilde by his side. The Professor followed them.

"What about me?" yelled Samuel. "What am I supposed to do?" He tried to start the car again. This time, the pedal-cyclist joined the motor-bike rider on the bonnet. Other car drivers joined in the argument.

"I think we should steer clear of that row," said Wally.

"It's typical of Brunhilde. Everywhere she goes, there's trouble!" said Spike.

"She rescued the Professor," said Doreen.

"We don't even know that he needed rescuing," said Spike. "He seems happy enough to stay with Harry Speakes and Brunhilde."

They caught up with the trio as they reached the corner of Crofton Road. "Stop," said Wally, raising his hand just as a policeman might. "What was the Professor doing in your car?"

"He collapsed in the street," Harry said.

"That's true," said the Professor. "And Harry's camera got run over!"

"Fortunately, my assistant, Samuel," as he spoke, Harry pointed back towards the brown car around which a pitched battle now seemed to be taking place, "was parked close at hand."

"He was driving me to Crofton Road to see Sticks. Brunhilde dropped the piece of paper with the address on it," the Professor said.

"We were having a talk when this young lady descended on us like a lioness defending her cubs!" Harry said.

"I thought you were kidnapping him," said Brunhilde.

"Kidnapping ?" said Harry. "Is that what's happened to certain members of The Tree-Tops? And don't give me any of your nonsense. I know that there is something wrong and, you can rest assured, that, once Harry Speakes is on the track of a good story, he will not give up until he's got the truth, the whole truth and nothing but the truth."

"We're at Number Seventeen," Doreen said, looking at the display of fruit and vegetables.

Peter rang the bell on a narrow door next to a pyramid of oranges and grapefruit. There was the sound of footsteps coming downstairs. Then the door was opened by a tall, thin young man dressed in jeans and an old white shirt. He seemed startled to see seven people on his door-step. Then he said, "Hello, Peter. Hello, Amanda. Please come in."

12
Brunhilde's Plan

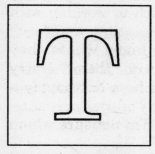

There were not enough chairs in Sticks's flat for everyone, so the young people squatted on the floor of the living-room which was long and narrow like a railway carriage. What little furniture there was, was plain and simple with no pictures or ornaments of any kind.

"I like to live like this," Sticks explained shyly, noticing how Harry and Brunhilde were looking around the room. "When I'm on tour or doing one-night gigs with the rest of the lads, we always stay in the most expensive hotels. This place reminds me of where I grew up in Australia. My Mom and Dad had a greengrocer's shop in Sydney."

"So you're just a simple boy at heart, are you?" asked Harry, taking a notebook out of his pocket. "In spite of all the money you've been making lately?"

"We don't do it for the money," Sticks said. "We do it for the music."

"Just like I do," said Brunhilde. "That's why I'm looking forward so much to working with Sticks and the others."

"Wouldn't you need to know where they were before you could work for them?" Harry asked. "Still, maybe Sticks here can supply a few answers."

Sticks blushed slightly. "I'm not sure where they are."

"But you're sure that they haven't been kidnapped?"

"Yes."

"What makes you so sure of that?"

"Well, because of what they said last Monday."

"Which was what, exactly?"

"Well, that things were getting them down."

"In other words, spoiled brat pop-stars run off in temper!" said Harry. "I'm going to tell the world that Scarce and Speedy and the Mole have deserted their fans and are not going to appear at the big concert tomorrow night!"

"You can't do that," Peter said. "You could cause no end of trouble."

"Which is what The Tree-Tops have been

causing me!" said Harry. "The only thing that will make me change my mind is if I get the full story on where the others have been hiding all this week. And I want that story no later than midnight tonight. Here's my card with the telephone number of where I'm staying." He put the card on the mantelpiece. "Now I'm going back to see how Samuel is getting on."

No-one spoke until they heard the front door slam. Then Peter said to Sticks, "Have you any idea where they might be?"

"No. I don't even know if they are together."

"What about Scarce's grandparents?" asked Wally.

"I've already telephoned them. Scarce hasn't been in touch. I tried Speedy and the Mole's families as well. There's been no word from them." Sticks ran his fingers through his hair. "Harry Speakes could ruin everything if he spreads the rumour that the concert is going to be cancelled. We've sold thousands of tickets."

"Perhaps the newspapers won't print the story," said Doreen.

"It's not just the newspapers. It's the television. Harry Speakes is on every Saturday morning. Anyone who is interested in pop-music listens to him!"

"Just one second," Wally said. "We're getting carried away here. Sticks, let me ask you a question. Do you think that Scarce and the others won't turn up for tomorrow night's concert?"

"Oh they'll be there all right. It's just that if Harry Speakes starts a rumour that they might not appear there could be real trouble at the stadium. The audience start to queue early in the day to get a good place. Some of the fans can be very excitable. If the police had to be sent for, the whole thing could be a shambles. The police might even make us call off the concert in order to avoid further trouble."

"That's where my plan comes in," said Brunhilde.

"What plan?" the Professor asked nervously.

"The plan that made me come around here in the first place! What would stop people rushing around trying to find out where all The Tree-Tops are?"

"Knowing where they are, I suppose," said the Professor.

"And how would they know where they were?"

"By seeing them some place, of course," said Doreen.

"And that," said Brunhilde, "is exactly what we are going to arrange."

"It seems to me that the Professor isn't the only person who has been out in the sun for too long," said Wally.

"Not so long that I can't think," said Brunhilde. "Harry Speakes has been following us not just because he thinks we know where Scarce and Speedy and the Mole are but because, for a long time, he thought that Spike and the Professor might be Speedy and the Mole."

Suddenly Spike knew what Brunhilde was getting at. "No," he said. "We'd never get away with it. You want the Professor and me to pretend to be Speedy and the Mole."

"And Sticks could be Sticks," said Doreen. "But who is going to be Scarce?"

"Why, I am, of course," said Brunhilde. "I'm the same height as he is. I can sing like him if I have to."

"Harry would guess what was going on at once," said Peter. "He's no fool."

"That's because he expects us to try and fool him," said Brunhilde. "But there must be other journalists who'd like a story about The Tree-Tops enjoying a night out at their favourite Greek restaurant on the night before their big concert."

"That restaurant isn't very brightly lit," Amanda said.

"And we know a few journalists who'd be delighted to share the story," said Peter. "But what happens when they find out the truth?"

"Why, we'd give them an even bigger story," said Brunhilde, "about Jenny being Scarce's mother and how she and The Tree-Tops are going to sing one of my songs on their very first record together!"

"It might just work," Peter said.

"What about clothes?" Spike asked. "Where would we get them?"

"The lads leave some of their stuff here," said Sticks. "It's hanging inside in the wardrobe."

"I think it's worth a try," said Wally. "In fact, I think it might be great gas."

Spike felt his stomach tighten. The hair on the back of his neck tingled. He realised that he was in agreement with Wally. It would be great gas! And what a story to tell Winky Murphy and the gang!

"Good. That's settled," said Brunhilde. "Let's have a look at the clothes. Then we'd better have a quick rehearsal of one of my songs in case we do have to sing."

"What about Granny O'Brien and the others?" asked Doreen.

"Just don't say anything to them," Brunhilde

replied. "We can go to the restaurant in different cars. I wonder where they are right now, anyway?"

The answer to that question was that the car in which they were, having moved very slowly along the High Street, was now part of the jam caused by Samuel and the motor cyclist. Alice sat as long as she could in the car. Then she could stand it no longer and got out to see what was going on.

Shortly afterwards, Martin joined her. Then Mrs Hurt. Then Granny O'Brien. They all got so involved in the argument, which became worse when Harry Speakes returned, that no one paid any attention to a group of people, with carrier bags filled with clothes, who walked quickly by in the direction of Jenny South's house.

Maria and Dolores were waiting anxiously in the hall. Amanda and Peter soon convinced them that everything was all right, that no-one would blame them for anything that had happened. "You may even take the rest of the evening off, if you like," Peter said.

Once the maids had left, Amanda and Peter kept watch in case the car came back. Upstairs in the girls' room, Brunhilde was teaching the others the words of her song about London,

which she had finished while selecting clothes
from the wardrobe in Sticks's flat.

Satisfied that they had a good notion of how
it should sound, Brunhilde said, "Now I think
the boys should go back to Daly Carson's
house. Doreen and I will meet you over there
as soon as Martin and the two Grannies have
set off for the restaurant with Peter and
Amanda. We'll collect Sticks and go on in the
second car. Alice will bring Harry Speakes."

13
At the Restaurant

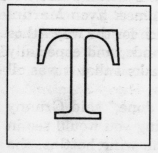

he Greek restaurant
was very dark, very large
and very crowded.

The owner hurried forward as Amanda and
Peter led Martin and Mrs Hurt and Granny
O'Brien in. "Good evening, Miss Richardson. And
Mr Arnew. It is a great pleasure to see you."

"Thank you, Athos," Amanda said. "These
are our friends from Dublin."

Athos smiled and kissed the hands of the two
ladies. "Such a delight to have you visit my
humble restaurant."

"I don't think it's humble at all," Granny
O'Brien said. "I think it's lovely."

"You are too kind," Athos said. "I have given
you the large table here in the corner. But
should there not be four more persons?"

"Actually, there are five more, one more

expected. They will be along in a few minutes."

"Good. Then, while you seat yourselves, I will get the waiter to set an extra place for your unexpected guest."

Mrs Hurt and Granny O'Brien could not stop looking around the place. Even Martin, who hadn't cared very much for the way Athos had kissed the ladies' hands, and especially Granny O'Brien's, had to admit that it was all "very nicely done."

"It's more than nicely done," said Granny O'Brien. "It's like something you would see in a film; the candles in the wine bottles, the little electric bulbs like stars in the ceiling, the flowers, the tablecloths, the lovely glasses and cutlery. Look, there's even a little platform over there for a band."

"So Brunhilde might yet get her chance to do a Greek dance," Martin groaned.

"We might all get a chance to do a Greek dance," said Peter. "It's a custom that everyone dances after dinner. There is actually a dance floor out in the garden. You can just see it, if you look beyond the dessert trolley."

"Well, well, our second dance in one week! First Wally's disco! Now a Greek place in London! And at our age too!" Silver bells tinkled as Granny and Mrs Hurt laughed at what Mrs

Hurt had said.

"Now, now, less of this talk about age," said Martin. "Many a good tune has been played on an old fiddle." He turned to Amanda and Peter. "The two of you seem to know a lot of the other people here. They keep waving and smiling at you."

"Yes. Our friends come here quite often," Amanda said. "And many of our friends are newspaper and television and radio journalists."

At that moment, the door opened. Wally and Doreen came in; behind them were four young people that Granny O'Brien thought she recognised. As she realised who they were, so did everyone else in the room. "It's The Tree-Tops! It's The Tree-Tops!"

Athos, followed by a crowd of waiters, was across to the door in less than two seconds. "Oh such a pleasure! Such a pleasure. We did not know we were to have the pleasure of your company this evening."

"We're having dinner with Miss Richardson and Mr Arnew," Wally said.

"Oh, and they did not warn me who their other guests would be."

"We didn't want to cause any excitement." The "Tree-Top" who spoke was wearing a boilersuit, torn at the knees, dark glasses and a beret pulled down over the forehead.

"Yes, of course, I understand, Mr Scarce. It is Mr Scarce, isn't it?" Athos said. "You see I know all of your names. My three daughters, they just adore your music. All day, all night, they play your records!" For a moment, it almost sounded as though he was complaining. Then he smiled again and said, "Please. Let me show you to your table."

Mr Scarce banged into several pillars and people as he walked across the room.

"Take off the dark glasses before you fall over something," Doreen hissed.

"Mind your own business," "Mr Scarce" hissed back in a voice very different from the one he had used to Athos. Then the voice changed again as he greeted Amanda and Peter. "Hello. How are you?"

"We're fine. You know everyone, I think."

"Yes, we do."

"Mr Scarce" took the seat next to Mrs Hurt. Sticks squeezed in next to Martin and sat looking shyly at the salt and pepper. Doreen sat next to Granny O'Brien with Wally and the other two "Tree-Tops" taking the other side of the table

"Sorry if we are a bit late," Wally said.

"Where are the children?" Granny O'Brien demanded.

"We're here," the "Tree-Top" facing her said.

Granny looked carefully at the two young men who were dressed as though for an outing to a rubbish tip. "Spike, is that you? And the Professor?"

"Shhhh!" hissed "Mr Scarce." "You'll give the game away."

"Brunhilde!" Martin was as confused as Granny. So was Mrs Hurt, who tilted Sticks's face up to what little light there was and said, "Doreen, is that you?"

"No," said Doreen. "I'm me over here. Why would I get dressed up as Sticks if he had to get dressed up as me?"

"Why would anyone want to dress up as anyone else at all is what I want to know." Granny O'Brien looked sternly at Wally. "You were supposed to be in charge "

"I *am* in charge," he said. "Trust me. Everything is going to be all right once Alice Hopper gets here."

Athos approached with a bundle of menus and passed them around.

"Could we have the kind of food they eat on the island of Kos?" Doreen asked, thinking of Imelda Flood.

"The island of Kos? You know the island of Kos? I'll bring you very special food from there. It's where I grew up," Athos said.

"I'll have the Kos special too," grunted Brunhilde.

"So will we," said Spike and the Professor.

"Why don't you all have it?" Athos said. "Even these lovely ladies will enjoy such wonderful food." Once more, he kissed the hands of Mrs Hurt and Granny O'Brien. "And some Greek wine. And perhaps grape juice for the younger people."

That suggestion suited everyone, although Martin declared, "That lad is too smart for his own good!"

Amanda laughed. "Mr Daly, you sound as though you are jealous."

"I'm not then," Martin replied, and was as silent as Sticks until the food arrived. It did indeed turn out to be delicious. There were stuffed vine-leaves, olives, fish, grilled chicken, stuffed tomatoes and at least five other dishes.

"I'm not sure what it is I'm eating," said Granny O'Brien, "but it suits me down to the ground."

It suited everyone else as well. After a few glasses of wine, which at first tasted very strange, Martin and Granny O'Brien and Mrs

Hurt were back in the best of humours.

Brunhilde didn't so much eat the food as give a performance, hunched over her plate, staring around her, suddenly waving at no-one in particular. Doreen kicked her on the ankle. "You're supposed to be famous, not out of your mind!"

"It's the way famous people behave in public," Brunhilde said.

"Sticks doesn't," Doreen said.

Indeed Sticks had remained silent, but he was clearly enjoying himself.

"Sticks is different," Brunhilde said. "He plays the drums."

"What has that got to do with it?" asked Spike.

"Everything," said Brunhilde. "I hope you haven't forgotten the words of the song!"

"What song?" Martin asked, in alarm.

"We thought we should be prepared in case they asked us to sing," said Brunhilde.

"You'll never get away with that," said Mrs Hurt. "It's one thing to dress up like The Tree-Tops, it's another thing to sound like them. Their records are probably played all the time on the radio since they got to number one. Everyone will know what they sound like."

"Yes, but only when they are singing the

songs that they have recorded. They wouldn't be expected to sound exactly the same singing a song that no-one has ever heard before."

"By which I take it you mean a song that you've written?" Martin asked.

"That's right. 'London, the City of Fear.'"

"Actually it's not too bad." This statement from Sticks made everyone jump.

"You mean that The Tree-Tops might perform it?" Peter asked.

Athos, the owner of the restaurant, heard the question. "Perform?" he said. "Your guests might perform a number here for us?"

"Well, if you insist," Brunhilde growled in her deep voice and was on her feet before anyone could stop her.

Athos jumped onto the platform and switched on the microphone. "Please! Your attention, please, ladies and gentlemen! We have a special treat. The Tree-Tops have agreed to per-form for us."

A ripple of applause went through the room as Brunhilde and Sticks left their table, followed by a very reluctant Spike and the Professor. Sticks tested the drum-kit. Brunhilde tested the microphone. Spike and the Professor wished the ground would open and swallow them.

"We'd like to do a new song for you," Brunhilde said, in her Scarce voice. "It's called 'London, City of Fear.' It is the first time it has been performed in public so, if Mr Athos could come and stand over here."

"Yes, of course," Athos murmured, moving to the place indicated by Brunhilde.

Brunhilde fished around inside the boilersuit and brought out the tape recorder that Wally had bought at Dublin Airport. "We borrowed this from a friend," she said, before Wally could complain. "He is over there next to Martin Daly, soon to become a star in Hollywood where his cousin, Daly Carson, lives."

A second ripple of applause went through the room. Several people produced cameras and started to take photographs. Brunhilde nodded at Sticks, who began to beat out the rhythm. Then Brunhilde began to sing with Spike and the Professor in the background.

London is city of danger.
And nothing will ever change her.

Then the new words were introduced.

Because with the danger
Comes the fear

That somewhere, near,
A man with a camera will go click-click
And say we are no-good.

People began to laugh. "It's not meant to be
funny," Doreen said.

"That doesn't matter," said Amanda. "They like
it and that's the main thing."

And it certainly did seem to be the main thing
and the laughter did not bother Brunhilde and
the boys, who were beginning to enjoy themselves.

As they began the third verse, Spike nudged
the Professor. "Look! Over there at the door."

Standing at the door were Harry Speakes
and Alice. Harry Speakes looked very cross.
Doreen saw him as well and said to Wally, "I
think the plan is working. Harry Speakes is
here and doesn't know what to say."

Doreen was right. Seen across the crowded,
dimly-lit restaurant, Brunhilde and the boys
did look exactly like The Tree-Tops. They were
managing to sound quite like them as well.
Harry recognised most of the journalists and
photographers there. His hope of writing a
story about how The Tree-Tops had run off
rather than give the Saturday concert was
vanishing.

Amanda said softly, "Even if he suspects

something is wrong, he won't even have those photographs he took to prove it."

"That's right," said Wally. "The camera got run over."

"What happens when the song is over?" asked Granny O'Brien. "Supposing he comes over demanding to know where The Tree-Tops have been all week?"

"Bouzouki," Doreen said. "Get Brunhilde a bouzouki."

A word with a passing waiter meant that, as Brunhilde finished her song to loud cheers, a bouzouki was handed to her. "I don't know much about Greek music," she said, almost using her ordinary speaking voice.

Athos came to the rescue. "But my musicians do! They would be so pleased to play with you."

Four musicians came out of the kitchen and joined "The Tree-Tops" on the platform. At first Brunhilde made hideous sounds but then she decided just to play the same three notes over and over again.

The audience began to clap in time to the music. The waiters stopped serving and moved into the garden where they began to dance in a circle. Athos called for everyone to join in.

As people left their places, the Professor said

to Brunhilde and Spike, "Now is our chance to get down from here."

"But I'm enjoying it," Brunhilde said.

"We've done what we set out to do, which was to convince Harry Speakes that The Tree-Tops have not run away. Now come on, please, Brunhilde."

With a great sigh, Brunhilde handed the bouzouki to a musician. Sticks left the drum-kit and followed the others down into the crowd, where Harry Speakes could no longer see them.

Alice said, "Do you want to stay and join in the party?"

Harry shook his head and said crossly, "No, I've better things to do!"

Alice said, "You surely aren't cross because things are all right, are you?"

Harry managed a weak smile, "No," he said. "It's just that, if there had been a good story, I would have liked to have written it."

He gave one final glance at the dancers in the garden, among whom were Granny O'Brien and Mrs Hurt and Martin and everyone else at their table. They were having a marvellous time.

"All right," Alice said. Then she was swept off by Athos, who soon had her dancing as merrily as anyone else.

14
Happy Endings

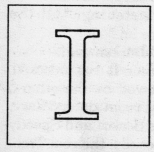t was very late when they left the restaurant. Athos refused to give them a bill. He said that he was honoured that The Tree-Tops had performed in his restaurant and handed the tape-recorder back to Brunhilde. More photographs were taken as they got into the cars and a promise given to Athos that he would be sent a special one, signed by all The Tree-Tops, to hang on the wall of his restaurant.

As they drove back to Sticks's place, Brunhilde said, "What an evening!"

"You were all great," Wally said.

"But what happens tomorrow?" Doreen asked. "What if the other Tree-Tops don't show up?"

"Maybe we could do the concert for them," said Brunhilde.

"You can't be serious," Spike said. "If the audience realised that they were being cheated, things would be worse than ever."

The car came to a halt outside the greengrocer's on Crofton Road. Sticks got out of the car. "Thank you for all your help," he said.

But Brunhilde wasn't listening. "All the lights in your flat seem to be on."

"I hope it isn't burglars," Doreen said.

Sticks ran to the narrow door. It was unlocked. He bounded upstairs, followed by the others, and threw open the living room door. There, sprawled on the floor, were Scarce and Speedy and the Mole. For a few seconds, the real Tree-Tops and the imitation Tree-Tops stared at each other. Then Scarce said, "It's what's-her-name and the two lads from Ireland, dressed up in our clothes! What have they been up to?"

"More to the question is what have you three been up to," said Wally. "Do you not realise how much trouble you've caused? Alice Hopper was on the verge of a nervous breakdown."

The three pop-stars looked ashamed when they heard this. Speedy said, "We never intended to be away so long. We borrowed a car to go to the west of Ireland but it broke down miles from nowhere. When we finally got it to a garage in this little town, the man there said he'd have it for us next morning. In fact, he didn't finish it until yesterday."

"You could have telephoned your mother," Wally said to Scarce.

"Oh you know that Jenny is my mother, then?"

"Yes. I also know that, if it hadn't been for these young people and Sticks, Harry Speakes would have written a terrible article about you."

"Not to mention stuff on television that could have ruined tomorrow's concert," said Doreen. "How did you get into this flat?"

"Sticks gave us a spare set of keys. But tell us exactly what happened?"

Scarce, Speedy and the Mole roared with laughter as the story of the last five days was told. Scarce, wiping his eyes, said, "All of you really have been brilliant. But now, can we hear the tape of this song of Brunhilde's?"

The quality of the sound was not very good. All the same, Scarce and the others were very impressed by the song. "We don't usually sing songs written by other people," Scarce said. "But I think we might include this in the concert tomorrow night."

From then on, Brunhilde existed in a world of her own. Next morning, as soon as breakfast was over, she was driven away by Ned to meet The Tree-Tops and go over the song with them.

That left Spike, the Professor and Doreen free to do the rest of their sightseeing with Wally. They went to Madame Tussauds and the Planetarium and the Museum of the Moving Image, all of which they enjoyed. Yet, in a way, it all seemed very quiet and ordinary compared to the previous day's adventures.

They arrived back at Jenny's house in time for tea. Not only were all four of The Tree-Tops there, but so were Jenny South and Daly Carson.

Jenny kissed each of them in turn. "I'm so sorry that we were so busy at the studio since you arrived, but we know all about how you helped Scarce and the boys. In fact, we've decided to tell the whole story to Harry Speakes just in case he finds out from somebody else."

"Are you also going to tell him that you are Scarce's mother?" asked Doreen.

"Yes, I am," said Jenny. "And about the record we are going to make together."

"They are probably going to use one of my songs," Brunhilde said.

"Oh that's great," said Doreen, giving Brunhilde a hug.

"But that's not the end of the news," said Granny O'Brien. "Jenny and Daly are going to get married."

"And that might not be the only marriage in

the near future," Martin said, giving Granny a wink.

Granny blushed the colour of a pale pink rose; then, seeing the look on her grand-children's faces, said, "Pay no attention to him!"

Those words, in a way, turned the tea-party into one of the happiest occasions anyone there could remember. Then it was time for The Tree-Tops to get ready for their concert. Alice was going with them to the stadium. Everyone else would travel in the two big cars.

As they went to their special seats in the stadium, many of the fans recognised Jenny and Daly, and waved and shouted. The two stars waved back. So did Brunhilde.

The concert began. The Tree-Tops were better than anyone could have expected. The audience loved them. Then Scarce introduced the song by Brunhilde and pointed to her. Brunhilde stood up and took a bow. The song began. As in the restaurant, everyone seemed to think it was funny and laughed and cheered and whistled when it was over.

"Congratulations!" Daly said to Brunhilde. "You could have a hit on your hands."

At the party after the concert in Daly's house, many people said the same thing to Brunhilde. One man wanted to talk to her about signing a contract. Wally interrupted this conversation by reminding Brunhilde that they had promised not to get involved in anything without permission from Dublin.

"Of course," said Brunhilde. "Anyway, I'm too young to sign a contract by myself."

Then she went off to make sure that she hadn't missed meeting anyone famous. Satisfied that she hadn't, she came back to Spike, the Professor and Doreen. She looked quite serious. "I just want you to know that I appreciate the way you've treated me. And put up with me. You are the best friends I've ever had and we are going to stay friends for the rest of our lives!"

The party finished. The guests went home. The two houses in Regent's Park were in darkness. Their occupants slept until ten o'clock the next morning, each one dreaming a special dream.

Breakfast next day (in the dining-room of Daly's house) was almost like the tea-party on the previous afternoon "What about Mass?" Granny O'Brien asked.

"No problem. We'll all go," said Daly. "Jenny likes the music."

After Mass, it was off down to the river Thames where Daly had hired a cabin-cruiser. The afternoon was spent drifting down to

Hampton Court and back to London. By early evening, even Brunhilde was exhausted.

"Our last day tomorrow," Granny O'Brien said. "How time flies!'

It flew even faster the next day as the four young people and Wally went shopping, buying things for themselves and presents for their parents. At five o'clock, tea was once more over. It was time to set out to the airport. Granny O'Brien and Mrs Hurt found the linen table-mats they had brought for Daly and Jenny in their suitcases.

"They are lovely," Jenny said. "I hope you will come and help us use them."

"We will, of course," said Granny. Tiny tears sparkled in her eyes. She hated good-byes.

So it seemed did everyone else as they hugged and shook hands.

"You don't mind if we don't come to the airport with you?" Daly asked, referring to himself and Jenny and The Tree-Tops. "We are expecting Harry Speakes to call to see us later on."

"Maybe I should stay," said Brunhilde.

"No," said Wally, very firmly. "We are all getting into the cars right now."

Martin held the door open for Mrs Hurt and Granny O'Brien. "It seems odd not to be going back with you to Dublin. But don't worry. You haven't seen the last of me."

"I think your granny is going to marry Martin," Brunhilde whispered to Doreen.

"Shhh," Doreen replied. "She'll hear you."

The journey to the airport took almost an hour because of the rush-hour traffic but, once they were all inside the departure building, everything went smoothly. They had a delicious meal on the plane. Then there was Dublin sparkling in the bright evening sunshine.

"I'm actually glad to be back," said the Professor.

"So am I," said Spike.

It was a feeling everyone in the group shared as they came out of the customs hall and found the real Professor O'Neill waiting for them.

Brunhilde couldn't help feeling disappointed that there were no reporters or photographers there as well but she decided not to complain.

As it was, there was attention and admiration enough when she arrived at the O'Neill house. All the grown-ups had heard The Tree-Tops sing her song and had seen her take a bow on television.

"Now all you have to take care of is The Brunhilde Brisk Show," said Mrs O'Neill.

Brunhilde had forgotten about the dance lessons she had been giving on Sandymount Strand but she decided that, just because she was going to be famous, she would not let Winky and Imelda and their friends down. "I'll see to that in the morning when I take Imelda back her bouzouki."

"Her mother has been around here looking for that," said the real Professor.

Word got around very quickly that the travellers were back from London. When Brunhilde and the Professor arrived next morning at the Tower, not only were Spike and Doreen waiting, so too were Imelda and Winky and their friends.

"Today is the day of The Brunhilde Brisk Show," Brunhilde announnced.

"Where is it going to happen?" asked Winky.

"Why, on the strand, of course," said Brunhilde.

"The strand?" said Imelda. "How can you have a show on a strand?"

"Just by having it there," said Brunhilde. "And, if we do it here each morning, before long the television people and the reporters and the photographers will all come back. I'll even include some of my songs. All you have to do is what I tell you to do."

The sound of Brunhilde's voice was having its usual effect on her listeners. Spike and the Professor and Doreen watched as the others followed Brunhilde out on to the strand and formed into lines. Brunhilde had brought the tape recorder to play the drum music. She also banged on the back of the bouzouki.

"I think this might be a good time to take Brandy for his walk," said the Professor.

Quietly he and Doreen and Spike slipped away; Brandy went wild with delight when he saw them.

"I'd like to see Brunhilde teach him to dance," said Spike.

"She doesn't need to," said Doreen. "He already has a dance of his own."

And off the three of them went, with Brandy dancing around and around them.

Spike and the Professor
by
Tony Hickey

Make way for trouble as in this, the first of
the series, our two heroes embark on a
series of disasters in their attempts to raise
money to go on a day trip.
Doreen is there as well. So too is Brandy
the dog.

The critics called it "Masterly, hilarious, a
comic masterpiece."

Children's
POOLBEG

*Spike and the Professor...and
Doreen at the Races*
by
Tony Hickey

What could be nicer than a day at the races
with Granny O'Brien? What could possibly
go wrong?
Just about everything is the answer,
especially when Brunhilde from America
tags along.
It scored 10 out of 10 on *Breakfast Club*.
The *Indy* loved it too.

Children's
POOLBEG

By the same author:

Joe in the Middle

Where is Joe?

"The kind of books that changes attitudes."

Children's
POOLBEG